The Life of a Trouser

by

Keith L. Wright

To My Dear Wife Diane who has given me her total support for many years.

Table of Contents

Cut Offs

Life as a Rag

To Paul

Dron

Keith Wright

She was pinkish, rather ragged at the edges, and certainly looked older than her years. We were close, so close we spent every evening hanging about, the two of us, sometimes even entwined, but nothing more. We were just thrown together, finding a kind of intimacy that hard workers, driven by others, found in their own limited, quiet moments.

Alone, pressed together one night, she told me she had spent her early life with a lady of the night, although she was quick to point out it was actually more day and night. I winced in sympathy when she softly confided in me that she had been treated badly, ripped and beaten regularly. She confessed she spent most of her time weeping, lying on the floor, trampled and degraded. She whispered softly she was often forgotten for weeks, then misused and twisted into unnatural positions but, mostly, discarded without any care for her wellbeing.

Once she was beautiful, that was clear to me, and certainly sophisticated, but an activity such as hers did not enable her to rise to the various attentions to which her friends, at the exclusive clothing store, had achieved. I could tell it was a great disappointment to her as she felt her pedigree was equally as good as theirs and better than many. Yet, despite her efforts in life, fate had cast its dark shadow. Hers had been a demanding life, exciting at times, and certainly not boring. Her mistress had sometimes treated her well and respected her qualities but, in a lady's busy life, she was certainly of no importance. She was not treated as a luxury garment, more an enticing adornment, to be cast aside when no longer needed.

The Beginning

I am however, getting ahead of myself as any story of a life should begin at the beginning and chart its way through a time passage, sometimes rough and sometimes smooth, but always swayed by unknown happenings and unguided forces.

As any young thing developing, it is difficult to say when the first knowledge of your existence and memories of your past, wheedle into your thoughts. I certainly have no memory of existing as the wool on a sheep's back or indeed the weaving of my cloth into a roll of undefined material. I guess this was the real start of my existence, the insemination of my weaves as in the sexual encounter of humans. I have no doubt fluid was involved but as far as the pleasure of enjoinment of weave was concerned I have never heard of the ecstasy purported to exist between the thrashing and fluid exchanges of humans.

Our gentleman took a great deal of time selecting our cloth as there was so much from which to choose. His choice was assisted by the following explanation regarding the typical fabric weights, tediously sung out by the diminutive, fawning tailor.

7oz – 9oz: Lightweight. Ideal for the height of summer here in the UK, as well as other hot climates abroad.

9.5oz – 11oz: Light to mid weight. Good for the transitional seasons (moving from spring to summer and late summer to autumn).

12oz – 13oz: Mid weight, but on the heavier side. A sound option for around eight months of the year. During the summer months can be a bit warm.

14oz – 19oz: Heavy weight. These are not as popular, but they're a tailor's dream because they make up so well, great on a cold autumn or winter's day.

With regard to the fabric types the choice expanded as the enthusiasm of the tailor's voice demonstrated a commitment to his trade.

Wool is the most commonly used suit fabric. The two main yarns produce worsted (where the fibres are combed before spinning) and woollen (where they are not). These can be woven in a number of ways, producing flannel, tweed, gabardine and fresco cloths, amongst others.

Cashmere or a cashmere-blend is considered luxury to the outsider, and as much as it is, it's worth knowing it can give an unwanted sheen to a suit cloth. Some people like the effect and it certainly is characteristic of Italian tailoring, but the traditional English way will have more of a matte finish to the wool

Linen screams summer. The one important thing to note is that it creases easily, and you have to buy into that fact. It is part of its unique character and is probably the only cloth type that is stylish to have a little creased up. It is also extremely breathable and tends to be far more porous compared to conventional wool construction and ideal for keeping cool when temperatures rise. It's advisable to choose reasonably heavy linen as this helps to retain its silhouette.

Seersucker is another favourite for the warmer months. It is woven in such a way that the bunching of the cloth gives it a wrinkled and 'puckered' appearance. Again, it is part of its natural charm and should never be pressed. Furthermore, it keeps the wearer cooler in hot weather because this puckering holds the fabric away from the skin, aiding air circulation.

An immense number of decisions for the gentleman to consider but as I grew up I believed my master well decided in his selections.

Our Combination

Jackie and I were perfectly suited; everyone always said we looked so good together. We had been designed and created in Saville Row, one of the best areas in the world for creating top quality garments for the discerning gentleman. We were subjected to four long sittings used for slight realigning and redesigning, making the perfect fit for our gentleman to wear with pride and total comfort.

I, of course, was the trouser, the mainstay of the ensemble, supporting my gentleman's private accoutrements, admittedly with the assistance of others, but displaying them in the subtle unrevealing but provocative way your own personal gentleman required. Some, although fortunately not my gentleman, preferred a bold protrusion, somewhat ostentatious to my tastes but as a subservient trouser we had always to follow the master's desires, a rule that I grew to understand all too often as our relationship mellowed. Straight and upright without horizontal creasing was our rule, together with a length just caressing the shoe and only occasionally revealing the sock.

My friend the jacket was clearly of matching material and was compelled to work with me in displaying the gentleman at his best. Jacky was my nickname for her. She often called me 'Strides' but I liked to be called by my real name 'gentleman's trouser'. My full cockney name is 'Round the Houses' but that is a bit long for most to bother with so I settle for 'Strides' but only to my closest friends.

My Jackie, the jacket, looked magnificent in her hand stitched lapels and double vent. She met me perfectly and caressed me warmly round my adjustable waistband. I had vertical pockets with a very slight flair in my legs giving my gentleman a slightly wider look than his skinny legs appeared. No turn ups, of course, just a straight, slightly reinforced bottom to make the perfect hang. I was not too tight, leaving just enough room for a lady to use her imagination when eyeing my carefully covered zip. We were both gorgeous and proud to be seen with our gentleman of success. We were of course very close, made out of the same cloth, and had a full and complete understanding. We were a British style suit which, although often described as best for the wider gentleman, worked comfortably on any body style.

Whilst in the cutting room I was surprised to hear that the double-breasted suit was a British invention but the classic "British" style suit was a significantly different style. The classic "British" suit is a single breasted suit, meaning it comes with only a single row of buttons down the front. It can be made in either a two-button or three-button style. It has the following features -

-Lightly or non-padded shoulders

-Highly tapered sides. This creates a "silhouette", and helps show off a thinner waist.

-Medium gorge. The gorge is the point in the suit where the lapels cross when a suit is done up. A low gorge tends to make one look shorter and bring attention to your tie; a high gorge brings attention up to your face. A medium gorge is normal on most suits. For a two button suit, it's about halfway up the front, for a three button suit it's about two-thirds of the way up.

-Dual vents. Vents are slits in the back of the suit. The dual vents originally sprang up because it allowed the suit to sit properly when you were on a horse. These days, it doesn't really do that much, but many people (my gentleman included) think that it helps the suit look better, at least from the waist down. Many suit manufacturers (including Italian) are now starting to incorporate this feature.

-Thin lapels. The lapel of the suit is the thin piece of fabric that runs down the front and is turned over.

-Notch or peak lapel. When you look at a lapel on a suit, there is a cut in them, very close to the top. A peak lapel has small triangle pointing up, and a notch lapel seems to have a small triangle cut out of it. While it is often personal choice, a notch lapel is considered more formal. There is a third type of lapel, called a "shawl" lapel, which just seems a curved piece of fabric on the front of the suit. This is seen exclusively on tuxedos, and is very rare these days.

A British suit may also have working cuff buttons, called a "Doctor's Cuff". They were originally made so that doctors could roll up the sleeves of their suit without taking off their jackets when they saw patients. This is now a rare and somewhat expensive option on a suit.

British suits are excellent for people who are a little bit wider. The thin lapels, small shoulder, and overall tighter cut of the suit tend to minimize one's width and accentuate one's height, perfect for making one a little taller and thinner. The strong taper also helps create the illusion of a strong "curve" at the waist, which can be very flattering to the wearer.

Clearly we were not created at this stage but once we were tailored to my gentleman's satisfaction somehow our souls were aware of such a potpourri of choices my master suffered before considering the trimming and tailoring of our shape to caress and support his body showing its best form and shape.

Our owner was a young man but clearly one of taste. He worked in a large open-plan office in London. We all rather liked this as it gave us the opportunity to meet other like-minded clothing, although we were a little guarded with whom we spent time. Being Saville Row, manners were important so a curt 'good morning' could not be avoided but fraternising with a Marks and Sparks we felt was somewhat below us.

The Boss's Story

I was ripped out of me box, the governor slinging the tissue to the floor and me full magnificence was exposed to the world for the first time. The gent shook me admiringly and held me to take a gander at me full shape and style. I could see the smile on his gob as he admired me quality. I could only agree with him as I felt the daylight straightening me wrinkles. I was later to learn that I was an arrogant sod but I always felt I deserved it as I knew I was an 'undergarment' as the posh called me 'of some style'.

Me gent then sniffed me for some queer reason but I was sure me only odour was of brand new making and no second hand pong that some pants throw off. Later I was to see him do the same to female undergarments, the dirty sod!

The next thing the governor did to surprise me was to ease off his rather well-worn boxers. Now I pride meself on being a pretty cool set of drawers. I am made to hug me gent's balls without squeezing them too tight, if you get me drift. Boxers are a bunch of useless tossers as far as I can see. They do nothing for feck sake. Any gent's loose dribble, and let's face it every gent has a loose dribble now and again, is left to roll down the leg and into the sock. They are a waste of space and should be destroyed at manufacture if I had my way. They ain't worth the cotton they were stitched with. Which brings me to the subject of thongs, now what the heck are they about? Or should I say not about. They are just a bunch of poncey straps that hold onto a pathetic ball bag that provides little or no support for the governor's tackle.

Anyway, the gent or should I now call him my gent, pulls his boxers off and without even a wet flannel of his kit he hauls me onto his self. It was a stink I was to become used to but, as a fresh virgin garment, I felt my innocence wither away in a haze of body odour.

Hugo Boss was a top notch maker of undergarments and gave all their garments a good training before they were issued into the real world. Of course I didn't need much teachin' cos I was a sharp style but it never 'urts to hear what the posh gits say. It was all 'you do this for your gentleman and you do that for him. Don't forget to be proud of who you are but show respect to the rest of the wardrobe'. All a lot of fecking bollocks if you ask me but I gotta say I was a bit wary about what I would meet in the wardrobe as I reckoned like I'd better be on the guard for anyone trying it on with me. I was the boss and I was going to stay the boss.

It was not much later that I was slung into this kind of cupboard with all sorts of other clobber. Taking a quick gander round I was soon aware of my innocence as I didn't recognise anyfink.

Feelin' a bit lost I decided to keep shtum and wait to see what occurred. Well it was not long after I arrived in this wardrobe fing I was politely greeted by this posh git called a trouser. My first thought was that we were not going to get on as he thought he was in charge but I was 'The Boss'. It turned out later that we ended up good mates. He introduced me to Jackie who I must say was a tidy bit of schmutter. Of course we couldn't go out together but I fought I might give her a tug in the wardrobe. I was then introduced to Mr Pink who seemed a bit of a Charlie Ronce but good enough. Later I did feel a tad worried as sometimes he seemed to tuck in a bit too tightly to me, but nothing ever appened.

My first impression of the governor was that he seemed a good enough bloke, clean and mostly caring of 'is clothes. He 'ad a good set of tackle which I guessed needed a bit of controlling. I was later to find they took a fair bit of handling by hisself and various female kinds that sorted out his kit. I fought the trouser should 'ave had more control of that sort of stuff but he told me one day that he had to let his gent do what 'e wanted.

Friends

Jackie and I were at first rather shy but, because of our identical origins, we knew we were made for each other. We were intimates and often discussed things that other clothing would not contemplate. I say discussed but, as identical cloth created by the same tailor, we needed no conversation, our thoughts just melded together as twins, although of course we were certainly not identical twins being a trouser and a jacket. I always thought of myself as the superior garment as my closeness to my gentleman's privates gave me an intimacy with him that Jackie could never achieve. She, however, felt that being worn at a higher level meant a superior position in the master's viewpoint. We hardly argued about such an issue but it was always a matter that prohibited the perfect bond, showing the gulf between us, a gulf that was to widen in the future.

One day, to my astonishment, Jackie, in rather hushed tones, asked me what I thought of the shirts we had been out with. I have to admit it was not a question I had really considered. I was simply in touch with the tail end of the garment and had little concern for his look and style. I know I was particularly impressed with a Jermyn Street shirt whose name escapes me. He had a nice long tail and if well wrapped round the rear, formed an excellent final barrier when our gentleman had been drinking beer and eating curry the night before. I suppose, apart from that, I had limited contact with shirts. I was to learn, however, that as time went on they would become a very good conduit between Jackie and me. I discovered they were a friendly bunch and willingly passed messages between us when direct conversation was not possible. Nevertheless I was somewhat surprised that, at such an early stage in our relationship, Jackie was so well versed in attributes of our close relations.

She was keen to sing the praises of the 'Hugo Boss' formal collection 'designed 'shirt she said 'to ensure a man is impeccably and appropriately dressed in every situation. A creator of exquisite style using quality materials, their collections benefit from expert workmanship to give a gentleman styles he would enjoy wearing, time after time.' As I later discovered he also created a superbly controlled style of under-short.

I was surprised at her knowledge but suspected she had seen this written on something that had been cherished in her inside pocket.

My suspicions were confirmed when she continued with enthusiasm about another shirt which was clearly her favourite. I was not a great fan as I thought him rather pompous and over stated. 'Mr Pink,' she strutted, 'was an 18th century London tailor who designed the iconic hunting coat. Meticulous attention to detail, exquisite manufacture and luxurious fabrics were the hallmarks of the brand and this is no different with the designs today. Sitting at number 85 on London's prestigious Jermyn Street, Thomas Pink is renowned for quality craftsmanship and specialises in formal shirting. This regular fitting classic is embellished with an understated hounds tooth pattern which will complement plain suiting and a rich coloured tie. A double cuff, hand-crafted semi-cutaway collar, signature pink gusset and a split yoke across the shoulder ensures traditional styling and lasting comfort.'

I had little to say on the subject at the time but made it my business to study the behaviour of all shirts as they rested intimately in my waistband. In fact as time went by I became a particular friend of Mr Pink and found him always well-mannered and kind.

One of my closest friends soon became 'The Boss' which I felt was an apt name for an excellent pair of cotton trunks, not the shirt who I came to despise. Occasionally I was paired with a 'Polo Ralph Lauren' or even a 'Gant' but they never seemed quite so snug with my gentleman. To me 'The Boss' was the best. He fitted perfectly, keeping my gentleman stable and saving him the need to occasionally make the adjustments that so many required when they failed in their duty. He was a well-made tight fitting pair of under-shorts. I was soon to find he saved me on many an occasion when a gaseous out-pouring had been followed by something more solid, although often more liquid than solid. He took it all, simply seeing it as part of his function. He was not always at his freshest but I guess, us being so close, I was more likely to notice it than others and gave due regard to his strenuous duties.

Another important part of his job was to catch the dribbles and the drips at the front. This saved me from unsightly wet marks and a build-up of unpleasant odour. He was not always successful, as a hurried folding of the gentleman's member, sometimes resulted in an early release of more than he was able to cope. Of course, there were several pairs of 'The Boss'. Such an active workload necessitated a good deal of laundering but they all worked hard and I admired them for their diligence. They were happy under-shorts and never complained, always ready to do their utmost to protect me and provide comfort, with style, for our gentleman. We were certainly close friends, spending many a tiring day undertaking our individual roles in seeing our master was well protected and comfortable at all times.

Another group of friends with which I was closely linked were a selection of socks. My favourites were the 'Polo Ralph Lauren' ribbed, the quiet subdued sock or sometimes Polo Ralph Lauren Rugby or Ted Baker Saxton Striped.

They all did their best to try to avoid the gentleman exposing his bare flesh.

In my opinion the 'Saxton Striped' was far too flash. He did not always keep up but poo- pooed my suggestion about garters or suspenders. He said he would be a laughing stock but I managed to stop myself from telling him that most of the wardrobe thought he was a joke anyway.

The one thing I became mildly jealous about the socks was that when our gentleman went to bed with a female, the socks were the only item of clothing he kept on. They therefore enjoyed all the fun, albeit in a non-inclusive role, though they said very little about it. 'The Boss' was also disturbed that he was never involved in such activity but I pointed out that, with his refined skills, he would probably make things difficult for the gentleman or indeed his lady, if that was her correct description.

It was only later in my existence that I experienced such a dreadful event. I thought of 'The Boss' but of course by then he had long since passed on.

Perfume

Now personally I am not a great fan of perfume or eau de cologne. To me there is nothing better than the pure smell of clean, well woven wool worsted. My gentleman however did not have the same idea, so I was regularly doused with one or other of his two favourite eau de colognes.

The EDC he preferred is found at the tail-end of the concentration spectrum, at around 3-8%, and is generally sold in large, 200 ml bottles. The stuff can be applied over and over via splashing or rubbing, as it only lasts about 2 hours. I was never happy however, when it was obvious he had a liaison with a young lady when an extra-large helping of the stuff was splashed over my fly zip. I was never quite sure of the purpose of such an action but I always had concerns that it could stiffen my zip or even rot my stitching.

His favorite essences were 'Cool Water' by Davidoff. I am told by Jackie, who is wise about all these things, that the *'skilful perfumer Pierre Bourdon'* made a decision to blend quite common ingredients, jasmine and sandalwood, with a few unique ones including lavender, cedar and musk. As a result, a *'pure contemporary masculine aroma'* became instantly recognizable.' Although there are similar products available on the market, this fresh aquatic fragrance holds a special place in my gentleman's heart.

The other, 'Drakkar Noir' by Guy Laroche, is probably one of the most powerful and real men scents ever created. "Drakkar Noir," Jackie lectures, "offers the *irresistible simplicity and lasting shower-fresh* scent that many women find so attractive! Created in 1982 by olfactory artist Pierre Wargnye, this fragrance became one of the club crawler's 'must have' attributes. Drakkar Noir smells classic, but not outdated. This is a powerhouse fragrance with incredibly strong projection velocity, designed for a mature man who knows what he wants!" I am not certain that applies to my master but I feel he has a good idea what he would like.

Skirts and Tights

A trouser is generally a gentle, well-meaning species of garment, possibly with the exception of denims jeans, as they are often called, but that is largely due to excessive in-breeding. We know what we are, just two legs meeting at the crotch and rising to the waist band. Of course various sub species have developed over the years but everyone knows what we are.

Now there is a theory (to which I do not subscribe), that we all evolved from the same species and then subdivided. As females originally wore a trouser they found the legs an inconvenience and so over the centuries for females the legs gradually withered and disappeared. So far such an idea has credence for me but the problem arises with the tights. If this idea is to be followed, tights being a garment with feet, were they original species and we all evolved from these? I just could not accept this as I felt no affinity with a close fitting stretchy product that was mostly worn by females and had little if any similarity to a sophisticated trouser such as myself.

Jackie always enjoyed winding me up because she knew how it affected my sensibilities. As far as I was concerned skirts were just trousers or shorts without legs, they were incomplete. They were just pieces of cloth wrapped round a body. There was no intimacy with the body and often, as far as I could understand, no contact. They had no shape and were of varying length from high to ground. Without legs, to me, they fulfilled no function at all. I did see them sometimes with tights, which at least had legs, but really a suit where they both compete with the same area of the body just did not seem to make sense. Tights themselves were a quandary to me. I understood there were so many species, from the simple tights and skirt which gave me some sort of clue, although in my view, the same function could have been performed much more effectively by a trouser.

There were tights that were worn without skirts but covered feet so were sort of trousers with socks. There were ski pants which were tights without socks.

Then skirts varied in style and, as I understood, were mostly worn by women however I was shocked to hear they were sometimes worn by men. My immediate reaction to such news was to enquire how there were capable of providing the comfort and protection of the men's accoutrements. I don't know, but I was even told once that Scotsmen wore such garments on a regular basis in cold climates where they wore nothing underneath for protection or control. I had not seen this myself and really did not believe it. I expect such a rumour would be concocted by a mischievous linen trouser, with little or no respect for the truth.

Now, as any well-bred trouser knows, there is no sexual differentiation between garments. Indeed in this modern era of relaxed standards it is not at all unusual for a gentleman's trouser to be worn by a female, a practice that I was to experience to my horror further in my career. The same situation applied to Jackie. I had simply chosen to denominate Jackie as a female to emphasise the closeness of our relationship not the differentiation of our creation and thinking. Indeed to coin an expression 'I don't wear the trousers, I am the trouser.' Many accused me of having deep pockets, too deep to show a generosity expected of a well stitched gentleman's trouser. I took most of the comments as pure fun from the lower garments as in my view generosity is a matter for the lower classes.

Going to work

I rather liked the underground journey as it meant I could meet trousers from all walks of life and exchange experiences of our master's antics and laugh at their mistakes. It often saddened me to hear how so many trousers were badly treated. They were worn home, thrown on a floor and left to wrinkle. Many of them were worn every single day without the opportunity to rest and restore the weave of their cloth. Some were not cleaned for six months at a time and were embarrassed about their frightful condition.

One day, in a particularly crowded carriage, I found myself pressed up against a rather tight fitting shiny trouser who, judging by the lack of frontal protrusion, I assumed to be worn by a woman. I suddenly realised that I was being pressed rather hard against this garment. Now I know a crowded train can result in a reduction in one's own personal space but it was rare that the press was so great that trousers were rubbed together. Suddenly, to my horror, I felt a movement in my crotch area and realised the intimacy was a deliberate ploy by my master. I frantically yelled at Jackie for an explanation. Her immediate response was that she was more than aware of the problem as her lapels were being rubbed against a rather low cut, well stretched t- shirt. My protrusion was expanding and I feared a sudden kick to loosen my expansion.

Fortunately at that moment the train halted and the crush subsided. My problem now was that to my extreme embarrassment my gentleman's mind was not focusing on the extension of his trouser and a substantial bulge was there for all to see. I did my best to rearrange matters so it was not so obvious but I began to hear comments from trousers nearby expressing their disgust at such behaviour. Again I expelled a frantic yell to Jackie to do something to wake our pervert from his dream but it was too late. A knee came hammering into my zip impressing the image of the teeth through Calvin and into my master's flesh. The swelling disappeared immediately despite the frantic rubbing I received to try to bring some circulation back to my master's tackle. Usually our journeys were less eventful.

Upon arriving at the office the procedure was the same every day. Jackie was carefully hung on a hanger and suspended from a coat rail. This gave her a clear sight of the whole office. I would go with my master to the coffee machine and rub gently against a rather nice tight fitting pair of denims. Now I am not a great fan of denim and do not believe the office is the place for such uncouth attire but the perfect shape of those tight curves was always a pleasant start to the day.

Following our fraternisation we moved to our desk close to Jackie. My gentleman sat at his desk and got on with whatever he does so, other than the occasional scratching and readjustments, I was left largely to myself. This was pleasant and relaxing but I was stuck under a desk so had very little to see and therefore had to rely on Jackie's observations.

Now the trouble with a jacket is that because of the position they hold on the body their view of life is very different from that of a trouser and, in my opinion, somewhat limited. They rarely look beyond their last button and have very little imagination or understanding for the more active part of a suit, which of course is the trouser. I had tried to impress upon her the importance of our joint relationship but I was never quite sure whether her observations of the 'upper half' as she insisted on calling it, were simply to infuriate me and tighten my seams, or a failure to understand my desire to appreciate the more mobile and interesting attire, the trouser.

Pocket

A pocket is part of a trousers' anatomy, or should I say, the trouser of a man, as I have heard of the odd ladies trouser that has no pocket at all. In my limited experience of life I have doubts as to whether such an item exists and if it does whether it is part of the same species or whether it has evolved from many of the varied ancestors of a woman's clothing. I am thus assured of the importance of a pocket or indeed several pockets in a trouser.

Generally a trouser has three pockets, two at the front and one at the back, as part of its makeup. Sometimes there will be two pockets at the rear but this is more the American style and considered de rigour in Saville row. Similarly a buttoned rear end pocket is not appreciated but it has become more acceptable. Personally I am not a great fan as to me it smacks more of the Cowboy image. There are always two pockets at the front sometimes with an additional ticket pocket which seems to have little value these days as such tickets that are possessed are in and out of pockets too frequently to be hidden in a small pocket and an Oyster card would not fit.

Thus we are talking about the two front pockets which can be vertical along the seams, parallel with the waist band or slanted. I am told by Jackie that this was a major stumbling block for my gentleman when he considered my design as he tested many different poses before he arrived at his decision. I am pleased to say that he decided on the vertical cut. This meant it was so much easier for me to keep a straight seam and remain tight throughout the day.

It was certain that in the early part of our relationship my gentleman was on the same wavelength as me and did not use my pockets at all. This was partly because in the creation of me to keep lines straight my pockets were lightly stitched. This flummoxed him for a while as he considered the pockets were for design only. Later the stitching loosened and he realised he could use his pockets for other purposes.

As our relationship progressed he started to crumple money into both pockets as his evening forays progressed to an extent that sometimes unsightly bulges appeared down my leg. I was content with this as part of my job is to straighten myself out and ensure my hang is correct. My pockets were never misshapen and my seams were still straight. Things started to change however when coins were thrown into the pocket. At night time, my gentleman would empty those coins from my insides and place them in a receptacle on his shelf, a manoeuvre that in itself was not a problem to me. I always managed to maintain the perfect press.

We had a crisis however one morning when my gentleman had been out late and overslept. He hurriedly showered and dressed and rushed off to work, an action that was not uncommon but, as we boarded the train, Jackie began to shift uncomfortably as if she was trying to cover something up. I growled at her to keep still and straighten herself up but she whined that I had problem. Then I discovered it, my pockets had been turned inside out as usual but in the rush of the mornings dressing they had remained inside out. Now people do not realise the embarrassment of such an exposure to a well-bred trouser. It is as if you are exposing your nakedness to the world, not quite your genitalia, but nearly as bad. I panicked and screamed at Jackie and Mr Pink to do something. Jackie just snivelled in panic but good old Mr Pink just said 'never mind old boy leave it to me.'

As I heard his voice I also felt a moving, stretching and squeezing and before I could decipher the actions, my pockets were drawn in by my master persuaded by the manoeuvring of the shirt. My relief was such I almost went limp for a moment.

The pocket issue however did not go away and in fact got worse. My master had developed a habit of talking with his hands in his pockets and sometimes jiggling his change. My fear of course was that I would suffer from permanent stretch marks which would be so unseemly.

Worse was to come as the change jangling developed into something worse. It was The Boss that first noticed it but I was aware something irregular was going on. We discovered the caressing of the loose change had built to caressing of his manhood. At first The Boss thought it was simply an itch that needed scratching. He therefore manoeuvred our master's genitals into a position where he was able to satisfy such a need. Unfortunately, we soon found between us that it was something worse than this as things or rather the thing sometimes swelled and was in danger of being observed by all.

The issue was raised at the next wardrobe meeting and a committee was set up comprising of myself, Jackie, Mr Pink and of course 'The Boss'. The Clark brothers wanted to join on the basis that if a hole appeared they could be affected and, on the same basis, a pair of socks suggested their involvement but their pleas were rejected.

We met on the next Sunday, our gentleman not being a churchgoer we had a day off as he spent his day in 'relaxed' attire. We tried to find a solution to the problem but there were no immediate answer and as with any committee arguments were tossed around, like the contents of a tumble dryer, but nothing were resolved. An adjournment to another occasion was inevitable.

Girlfriend

As a young trouser I know little about relationships. I know I have a relationship with Jackie but that is simply because we are made of the same cloth and therefore go naturally together. I also have a relationship with underwear such as 'Calvin Klein' or 'Hugo Boss' or even for a 'lack of clean stuff day' Marks and Spencer. This however is clearly very different from the connection with Jackie as we are just very close and in some ways, I rely on her. As far as socks like 'Polo' or 'ribbed' are concerned and even more with shoes with whom we are acquainted but not close.

Intimacy is a word I hear about relationships but I do not really understand the importance. I could only say that I am regularly rubbing against Jackie and The Boss so, maybe I am intimate with them. It does not seem exciting as I believe the word means but I can only accept that a trouser is not generally woven for excitement.

My knowledge of life however, expanded one summer's day when I became aware that my gentleman was regularly walking out with a tight pink trouser. I did not know how long this had been going on or how my intuition had interpreted this as something different. A trouser is a different garment from most, I guess, because of his intimacy with his master and his connection with the world. We do not have eyes of course but revel in an unusual intuition and strength of feeling. Sometimes, we could say, we can see as well out of our backside as our flyside but our flyside is the important view of the world but with a backup from behind, should our view be obstructed. In fact the combined senses of a trouser have an ability to assess a situation, whether good or bad, and react in a way that no other garment can.

The view of a trouser is of course very different from its owner. Apart from anything else we are lower down in the viewing spectrum and need to react very differently in any situation. My impression therefore of the tight pink trouser was one of impertinent carousal, but nothing I would understand as intimacy.

One fine summer evening, after work, my master and his companion seemed to be strolling in unison along sun dappled lanes, occasionally brushing together in an embarrassed emotion, and then separated leaving us trousers to continue the appropriate line of direction. I, of course, had no feeling for the pink trouser and found her somewhat irritating in her lack of control of her direction.

All this, to me, was an acceptable part of my duties as a trouser but the small dog that accompanied us on these perambulations scrambled my weave to an intensity that I found difficult to control. He, or it, seemed to be a part of the pink trouser as it was always close to the trouser leg. It also appeared to enjoy rubbing itself against the pink leg sometimes with a frantic motion that I felt was far from appropriate. The feeling towards me, however, was more that of aggressor, trying to intimidate me into making an error of judgement and pulling my gentleman in the wrong direction. I, in my turn, attempted to kick the hound as hard as I could to deter it from its efforts. Clarks, my companion shoes for the day, were not aware of the issue and so were somewhat reluctant to assist me in my mission. The consequence therefore was that the mutt was little deterred. In fact, sensing my irritation, it decided to tear at my leg and then urinate on Clarks! Well, I have never seen a well-bred shoe act so violently. Without warning the well-made shoe raised itself slightly off the ground and reversed as if stringing an arrow, then, with the force of a rocket, released itself into the dog's side. The kick inflicted on the creature's ribs sent it yelping to the pink trouser in terror. We were, however, not troubled again. The heroism of the Clark brothers was raised at the next wardrobe meeting and they received a commendation for their bravery.

My gentleman's relationship with the pink trouser seemed to blossom. I was however sometimes aware that this same pink trouser was worn, without cleaning, on far too many occasions. I also realised it was being supported by nothing but a pink thong or sometimes, simply nothing and so it absorbed the persistent perspiration of a female kind and, despite the drenching in powerful deodorants, had a malodorous stale scent that turned a well-bred trouser like myself somewhat nauseas.

One night my gentleman was suited with Jackie and myself and we felt especially sharp in our enthusiasm for a night's enjoyment as we arrived late at a darkened night club. Now as a young, fairly athletic trouser you would think that dancing was something that I enjoyed but I regret that it is not the case. I am a little too stiff and starchy for such activity. It was thus that I was pleased to find myself vibrating with loud music but standing at a bar with no suggestion of movement to any active beat. I was aware the pink trouser was not in sight but could only feel pleasure at such absence being never enthused by her company.

Our stillness, sadly, was not to remain as we were approached by a short skirt that seemed to rub against me in a less than maidenly way. I was pleased however to spot immediately that some form of underwear was apparent. The effect of her excitement was to raise my gentleman's enthusiasm for activity and he joyfully followed the excited skirt to the dance floor. The music was fast and the beat was heavy so we soon found ourselves acting athletically frantic, movements to me that seemed far remote from dancing.

Now as I have said this is not my favourite activity and my sharp creases do not make it easy. As soon as we started I very quickly became aware of my companions for the night, a pair of Nike trainers. I recalled shuddering in the bedroom at such a combination of a Saville Row suit and trainers, no matter how expensive, as I remember us being introduced to my gentleman's body. Nikes, in my view, were still common and certainly out of style with a trouser such as me.

As every trouser knows, trainers, particularly Nikes, are very excitable items and my footwear, due to its enormous cost, was of the exceptionally excitable type. Before I knew where we were we were moving in all sorts of directions at rapid speed that, as far as I could tell, bore little relationship to the beat. I felt a sudden slide to the left followed by a twist and rapid move to the right, gyrating to a high kick and split. My seams screamed at the effort and I was afraid they would break in the energetic movement. My gentleman was sweating profusely and my crotch was starting to become damp. I could feel Jackie pounding on my back screaming at the lack of regular movement. Fortunately, after a while the music stopped and we moved back to the bar, apparently without the short skirt. My relief was profound and, while my gentleman caught his breath, I fumed about the antics of the trainers and vowed to raise the issue at the next wardrobe meeting.

We relaxed and my seams softened leaving me to straighten my creases and resume the demeanour of a gentleman's trouser. It was then that I saw the pink trouser sidling up to me, in a fawning sort of way. We sat side by side uncommunicative for a while as our owners conversed in whatever way owners do.

After a while I felt an excitement in the Nikes and, despite my reluctance, found myself propelled once again into the throng of gyrating bodies. I was relieved however to note the tempo of the music was considerably slower and, despite the trainers attempts at enthusiastic pantomime, we slowed to a gentle rhythm. This I found far more to my liking and relaxed into a soft movement of my creases in time, well sort of in time, with the music.

I did not immediately notice that the pink trouser had moved close to me and in fact was pressing itself against me. I discovered the combined movement of our owners was now joined as one and we slowly swayed to the sound. The two of us, trouser to trouser, my gentleman and his friend pressed cheek to cheek, hard against each other in a romantic warmth of rhythm.

Now I am a young trouser, a virgin some would say, so the sudden swelling along my zip surprised and began to concern me. I am made for my gentleman to hang loosely to the right and this movement out of position I found difficult to accept. It grew and it grew to an extent that I was afraid my zip would break. My concern grew with the expansion and my seams stiffened with fear. Worst came as a hand somehow managed to slip down my waistband and under 'The Boss'. It touched the snake-like expansion and began to rub it. I screamed in fear as I was simply not made for this movement and was sure there was no room for this fondling. Surely my gentleman must be aware of this intrusion and the possible consequences. At the very least with all that activity I was sure I would end up with permanent stretch marks and possibly split seams. As my terror built I was pleased to find that the music had stopped and we were moving once again to the bar, the investigating digits having removed themselves.

It was only a few years later that I understood the nature of this gentleman's activity and, although I did not suffer from stretch marks as such, as I grew older my frontal area certainly expanded over time to allow a flexibility for the intrusions and expansions. I never however believed that this was any procedure in which my gentleman should participate, but he clearly did not agree.

At the bar we slouched together and caressed leg to leg in an intimate way. We soon moved outside and I noticed the pink trouser was giggling suggestively as we slid into the back seat of a taxi. It was then that terror struck me again as my zip was undone and my gentleman's huge member was released from its constriction and exposed to view. I was desperately dragged down by a frustrated female frenzy for fornication, whatever that was, in the back of a taxi.

What happened next was way beyond my understanding but once reaching our destination I was relieved to feel that everything was back to normal size.

Gay Experience

One night my gentleman surprised me by going home straight from work rather than his usual 'couple of beers' with his colleagues. He seemed slightly nervous for some reason, a tension only a well-fitting trouser such as me can sense. It was no surprise to me then, that on arriving home Jackie and I were removed. However rather than idly thrown on the bedroom floor as usual we were carefully sprayed with a little water, a ritual I am told will allow the creases to drop out and the fabric set firm. Personally I never believed in this as I thought the only way to sharpen a trouser was to gently steam out the creases and allow the garment to hang over night. I, of course, had no say in this matter so after an over enthusiastic dampening I did my best to straighten up on the hanger and force out the creases with the moisture.

I had assumed this was the last I would see of my owner this night as he would usually slip into more casual attire that, personally, I would have no desire to make their acquaintance. I considered they were a totally different class of garment from Jackie and me. It was therefore a surprise that a few hours later we were removed from the wardrobe, shaken out and carefully stretched out on the bed.

As I lay there, straight and relaxed, I noticed an entirely different form of gentleman's underwear being carefully adjusted to my master's private parts. Jackie, who knew a lot more than I did, started to laugh. As my confusion grew she laughed louder and louder. "Well my friend," I heard her guffaw "You have got some fun in store for you tonight!" I pleaded for some form of explanation but all Jackie could say between her shivering mirth was that I was about to meet my first thong.

My shock at my extremely intimate experience of a thong was beyond my darkest imaginings. My proximity to my master's nether regions was an intimacy with which I found difficult to deal. Calvin or The Boss were always my support, my protection against unwanted intrusions, but this slutty thong did nothing. Well, maybe, that is not quite true as the front support seemed to be relatively adequate and, as I understand, quite sexy, but the rear was almost non-existent. I could not believe, when I was hoisted up and fastened, the proximity to my gentleman's flesh was greater than it had ever been. Certainly at the rear I was part of him, his sweat and the smell of extensive body rub, together with other odours that I found difficult to distinguish, were also mine. My gentle fragrance of a well woven cloth was almost obliterated.

As I was trying to relate to this new experience I felt a white vest being tucked into my waistband. Once again this was a slightly different garment as, usually, my gentleman was satisfied with a well-produced shirt. I braced myself to see which shirt was going to join us but suddenly felt Jackie being slipped over the vest. I began to panic as my master started to leave the house. 'Surely', I gasped to myself, 'he could not have forgotten to put on his shirt?' As far as I could tell he was not drunk so maybe his mind had gone. I tried to contact Jackie but without a shirt to act as a conduit we were unable to communicate well enough but I could feel her horror. There was nothing of course we could do but wait in trepidation for the terrible embarrassment when someone pointed out the error to my gentleman. I certainly felt for his extreme horror as he would undoubtedly feel once his error was discovered and he was forced to run home in shame.

This, however, did not turn out to be the case. After a long taxi ride we arrived at a strange club with which I was certainly not familiar. Once again I believe I felt my master was somewhat nervous but it was not totally clear through the somewhat fickle feelings of this silk thong. There was certainly plenty of sweat seeping into my stitching and much anxiety permeating from my fellow garments. We braced ourselves for the inevitable rejection from the club and the ribaldry from all, following my master's faux pas over the shirt, or lack of it.

We entered the premises which were dark but garishly decorated in a way that I had never seen before. There seemed to be a vast selection of trousers, clearly expensive but without my superior weave. Most seemed too tight on their masters and some appeared to expose far too much in their figure-hugging stance. I gasped at one particular trouser that was totally exposed at the rear, revealing a mystifying extent of bare buttock.

To our surprise, and maybe a little relief that the ejection did not happen, my owner was welcomed into the club with a great deal of touching and patting from far too many people, in my view. Much of the patting seemed to be on my rear end where there was no supportive padding provided by this dreadful thong. I also quickly realised that many of the male occupants were dressed in a similar way to my owner, no shirt.

It was not long before we were dancing. This was no surprise as it had become a part of his natural behaviour when he heard certain music. He had developed a liking to exude energy with exaggerated arm gyrations and uncoordinated hops and jumps, creating vast amounts of body heat and a certain amount of odour. Tonight this made life particularly difficult for me because unlike Calvin or The Boss, with whom I could work together to control any misguided movement of my gentleman's private ends, this thong had no idea what to do and in fact seemed to show little interest in his expected undertaking. He seemed to be reasonable controlled at the front although I did experience a couple of pop outs that I managed to slip back into place on my own. The major problem, however, was at the rear where there was absolutely no protection at all. So far we were fine but as an experienced trouser I am more than aware of what can occur later in a night of dancing.

Quite suddenly I was relieved to hear that the music had slowed down and my owner was caressed into a slow rhythmic rocking, pressed tightly against the body of another person. I was now very familiar with this process and was not surprised to feel my master's bulge pressing against my zip. My gentleman was clearly out for some fun and I could imagine the rest of the night with myself and Jackie being thrown on a bedroom floor amongst well scented ladies underwear. Our experience had taught us how such garments were small minded and frilly and they would have no conversation other than how important and expensive they were. They would be extremely skimpy and pea brained wittering about nothing in particular, causing total irritation to us well-bred attire. Even the more expensive lingerie seemed to have little to say worth noting.

However, as I prepared myself for the night's events I became aware of an unfamiliar lump pressing against my master's erection. Slowly the dawn of fearful recognition started to overcome me. I began to hyperventilate in a way only a trouser can. I screamed for Jackie but without a shirt to help we were left in our own separate worlds. I had no idea what Jackie was experiencing but as the vest was pulled out of my waistband I even sought comfort from the thong. Isolated, my only solution was to calm myself and consider the possible outcomes and hope for the best.

There was no doubt in my mind this was two men together, looking to pleasure each other. My master had turned, I shuddered. I wasn't altogether sure what that meant but I had heard the sneakers giggling about such things in the wardrobe. How could I deal with this with my acquaintances in Jermyn Street or Saville Row, I was sure I would be a laughing stock! I was also totally ignorant of the procedure for this and wondered whether it was similar to the heterosexual requirements. This was straight forward as we were simply removed as quickly as possible and thrown on the floor. Whatever the required mode of behaviour I was determined to undertake my task as any gentleman's trouser should.

I hoped my duty would be obvious but as I contemplated my role with trepidation, I became more aware of the firm members becoming more frantic in their frictions. I started to scream like a girl, in my panic and suddenly became aware of the opposite trouser that was rubbing up against me.

"This must be your first time," he said, with a slightly affected lisp. "Don't worry it will all be over soon. You may feel a little damp afterwards but it will probably be an early night. Oops there we go! Nice to meet you anyway, maybe we will get together again sometime."

The Thong

The gay experience was fading from my mind and we slid back into out routine. Our day was the same as ever, a working day, no more, but my experiences were certainly different at present. My man had persisted with the thong and when my gentleman bent down I found myself screaming 'no more! I am disappearing to places more intimate than I had ever imagined. I am forced into dark, dank crevices which released a distemper that no gentleman's trouser should ever experience.' 'No do not bend down further' I screamed, as my strongest bonded seams were burrowed into my gentleman's behind. As we settled to a more even, seated position, I can hardly say I was comfortable as the thong exposed me to a proximity of my gentleman's orifice that I would rather not have experienced. Even my frontal regions were not as supported as 'The Boss' had achieved. Also I could not help noticing my gentleman's regular adjustment of his equipment in his attempt at trying to make it settle into a more comfortable position.

As I grumbled about this situation I suddenly realised that my man was sweating into my cloth. Now this had not happened before, except of course in the nightclub. This was a job for 'The Boss' to protect me from the malodorous oozing of my gentleman's privates. The thong simply failed in this job and just further contributed to my loathing of such an inadequate garment. At least,

I thought, with such infected moistening I would have the benefit of a pleasant dry clean tomorrow to remove the smell of the day's exposure.

Next morning however I was horrified to find that I was on duty again. The thong had been replaced but what good that did I failed to understand. It was thus that for the next 2 weeks I became ever more caked in my master's sweat. I was embarrassed at the stench I exuded and was finding it increasingly difficult to maintain my creases and fight back the wrinkles. The thongs, with whom by now I had reluctantly become acquainted, described this as a musk which many a gentleman liked to exude to attract a female. I just found this impossible to believe as, to my knowledge, and as part of my initial induction training at the tailors, I was taught that a gentleman would attract a female through his clever language and the impressive hang of his trouser. This was a task of which I was always proud and considered myself somewhat of an expert in such an area.

With a thong there seemed to be nothing of it, particularly at the back where the gas would escape and, without the protection of a layer of shorts with whom I was very close, there could be a disaster and possible a seam split or even worse, a follow through. Thankfully this experience was rarely repeated but it left a lasting scar in my seams.

Conference

Conferences, according to my gentleman, are boring affairs but must be attended. We knew the procedure and thus, after a 3 hour drive, we arrived at the smart conference centre. A new venue changed from our usual expensive hotel and, although opulent, had an air of the outdoors in its look.

The usual evening buffet with good food and quality wine flowed through into the late hours. This was a time I quite enjoyed as it gave me the opportunity to meet quality trousers of my own tailoring some of whom I had known for a few years. Most, however were new to my acquaintance and, whilst a little exuberant in their enthusiasm, as all youngsters are, they sometimes had new thoughts and ideas that I appreciated. We circulated the gathering and joined various groups making sure not to stay too long, thus ensuring all colleagues and, more importantly, management were aware of our presence.

I remember one occurrence when we approached a smart trouser, obviously purchased for the occasion. I immediately recognised the good quality wool worsted.

As we drew up close, however, I suddenly cringed as I recognised a Marks and Spencer. Now some may accuse me of being a snob but I reject that criticism. I like to think I can get on with anyone, denims possibly excepted. I determined in the general fraternity of the evening to engage the trouser in conversation with a casual introduction of myself and my gentleman. Well I should not have bothered. This trouser was so off the peg that it had virtually no conversation at all and certainly no manners.

The evening dragged on and although most people do not appreciate that trousers get tired, standing for hours without the alcoholic fortification my gentleman enjoyed, causes problems. Now whether it was the alcohol or my tiredness I don't know but I was very much aware that I was not as steady as I was at the beginning of the evening.

At last we went to our room in a rather staggering sort of way and I was delighted when eventually my gentleman managed to heave me off his legs by lying on the floor and waving said limbs in the air. I was then carefully placed in the trouser press. My master however was not capable at that time of a great deal of care and, whilst I enjoyed the warm caresses of the press, I knew the next morning, in just 3 hours, it would result in me having creases that should not be there. An embarrassment of course but I was experienced enough to know that it was a shame felt by most trousers at conferences.

Breakfast time arrived shortly afterwards and I was hurriedly hauled on and became well aware of the smell of stale beer, wine and garlic, intermeshed with the odour of hotel body rub.

A breakfast of eggs, bacon, sausage and plenty of baked beans was washed down with several cups of strong coffee by my still inebriated master. Us clothes knew what trouble such a concoction could cause but were unable to do anything about it. We just prepared ourselves for certain eventualities.

We repaired to the conference hall and the usual droning started. As we feared, such amounts of food caused my gentleman to become sleepy and it was all we could do despite itching, tightening, squeezing and moving, to keep him awake. Suddenly we noticed a change and, at the same time, heard the mention of staff annual bonus. Immediately my gentleman's buttocks clenched to a firmness that took me and The Boss by surprise. We worked together to steady matters and at last almost relaxed. Now we were not aware of what was said but it had a major effect on the food that had been consumed about an hour earlier.

It started with a gurgling, bubbling sound which moved to a sort of swishing wave like motion. It was The Boss, as always, that received the restraining buttock tightness but was soon overwhelmed by a soundless but strong wind chime. This continued for a while and eventually hit me with an overwhelming force. My gentleman, we knew, was in trouble and despite our efforts we were afraid that we could be involved in a major and unpleasant incident. Unknown to us, as we were otherwise occupied, the droning stopped and my master rapidly exited the room heading straight for the toilets. We were rushed into a cubicle and were franticly stripped to the floor, followed by the sound of a gush of unorganised effluent.

We had, however, saved our embarrassment but as my gentleman relaxed in his relief I discovered in his enthusiasm he had broken my zip. The adrenaline having left me, I began to feel the discomfort but I did my best to hold myself together and hope no one noticed.

Despite this, the last afternoon always promised to be relaxing as we enjoyed the end of the conference and looked forward to the return home. Now whether my gentleman did not receive the email or did not read it we will never know, but the format for this year had changed. All those present were asked to bring outdoor clothes for an afternoon hike. It was thus that my gentleman was the subject of great shame and ridicule as we set off in the pouring rain, with him being the only one dressed in a suit.

Now a trouser cannot see into the future and unless your gentleman is drunk he does not talk to you and even then the comments do not make much sense to a simple trouser. We, and I mean my gentleman's entire ensemble, were not prepared for what was to happen next.

The Clark Brothers were the first to discover the problem as we sludged our way through muddy paths and they became smothered in a damp slime. They said little but we were all aware of their discomfort. The Clark boys were a well-made shoe and could handle most things without complaint but this was too much, even for them.

The Ted Bakers of course were very different. We waded through a shallow stream that was enough to cover the Clarks and overflowed into them, wetting the Teds. At first we were shocked by a yelped enthusiasm as the Teds experienced their first ever cold soaking as the clear cool stream engulfed them. This was soon to change as the water sloshing about the inside of the Clarks became warm and the whining Teds became sodden with what was now turning into a pungent froth. Their complaints just annoyed us all and we were agreed that once again their poor behaviour would be raised at the next wardrobe meeting.

My situation was precarious as mud splattered my nether regions but, being a tough trouser, I managed to keep myself together. I was determined not to be sent for invisible mending again.

Jackie, although the least affected, only suffering the occasional swishing branch, just like a typical jacket, was moaning all the time. I tried to keep her calm and gently caressed her where we touched but, jackets are jackets, and if they are not happy they feel the need to let everyone know.

That night when we eventually arrived home we were all thrown on the floor for, as we hoped, we would receive a proper appraisal tomorrow. Although it was nothing to do with me I was keen to assess the damage and see if I could manipulate our gentleman into taking the right course of action in the morning. He was a fairly considerate owner so I was confident a subtle push in the right direction would work.

I was quick to consider Jackie and a gentle calming found her quiet and asleep. I knew she needed a good clean and was confident the two of us would be recuperating at the cleaners very soon. My tragedy was nothing more than a thick coating of mud and despite a few brambles hanging on to my legs and my knees scraped by the regular falls in decaying gunge I felt confident of my survival.

The Teds were still whining but it was clear to me that a good Aerial soak would revive them to their usual annoying selves.

The Clark boys were more of a worry, however. They were badly scuffed and scratched. Their leather uppers were distorted by the brambles and their soles were encrusted with small stones and thorns. They were soaked through and if not dried properly might possibly be infected with a mould growth that would damage them for ever. There was nothing for it but they had to go a specialist cobbler. A High Street practitioner was not sufficient as most of these knew little about saving the lives of a quality shoe. These people were happier to condemn the shoe to oblivion and replace it with a new inferior product. I was not going to let the Clark brothers suffer this. I knew they were tough enough to recover and I was determined to ensure proper corrective surgery was employed to bring them back to their functional best.

My encouragement worked and it was not long before we were all regenerated to almost new and were happy to attend the wardrobe once again and take our rightful place.

The Fight

Now as you know dear reader if you have read this book from the beginning, which of course you should have done to get the full journey of my life in perspective, you will have noted that I do not stray from the narrative. However this one event was of such significance in our lives that I need to extend my tale into the here and now. It bonded us as a team and showed that clothes, like humans, are capable of significant acts of bravery, way beyond people's understanding.

"Oops," slurred my gentleman, "come on trouser keep me going forward." He had been drinking. I knew this because he never talked to me unless he was in his strange world of confusion and make believe. I never thought he knew I understood him or indeed expected me to answer.

"I am doing my best," I mumbled, as I tried to straighten a sideways move projected on me without any discernible motive. A sudden attempt to stagger me backwards forced me to stiffen my seams and keep my gentleman from falling. We were not really making headway and I had resigned myself to a difficult night.

Suddenly after another pace backwards I heard Jackie scream.

"What on earth is the problem?" I shouted as I failed to stop another pace backwards.

"Help!" she cried. "They have me by the lapels and are shaking our gentleman!"

"Can't you stop them?" I said impatiently, not knowing at this stage of what a jacket was capable.

"I will try," she whimpered. 'But these hands are firm and rough and I am frightened they will damage me."

It was all I could do to control my annoyance at these pathetic ramblings as I had my work cut out trying to keep the master upright, a far more important job in my view. I did not say this of course as we were, after all, both made of the same material and were expected, or indeed intended, to work together.

"Do you not have arms?" I questioned, as the screams grew louder.

"Yes I do," she said "but I am not really sure how to use them."

"Look, did you not go to initial jacket induction the same way I went to trouser training?" I shouted crossly.

"Yes," she whimpered, "but I have forgotten most of it, feeling it of little use in this modern sophisticated world.'"

My seams were tightening in anger and I yelled, more harshly than I should. "Well now is the time to strain your button holes and remember what you were taught. Our lives could depend on it."

At this point I heard a shout from 'The Boss'. "Quick trouser, while you two are passing the time of day I need a bit of focus here! Get your arse in gear!"

"I am sorry my friend, but Jackie is being a little immature and panics easily."

"Well she is very young and quite sexy in a jacket sort of way," said The Boss, surprisingly calmly, "so you need to give er some room, tosser."

'OK! OK!" I said, "But what is your problem?" I said more irritably than I meant.

"Well I am staring to feel strong rumblins at the back, know wot I mean, I may struggle wiv em. I ave managed to hold fings OKl at the front but it is sapping me strenf. I am knackered already"

"I don't know what you think you've been doing but it certainly hasn't worked. I'm soaked down here! How trouser hasn't noticed it going down his leg I don't know. Probably too busy chatting up Jackie!" moaned Ted.

"Oh of all the socks we have to get you, the smart arse. Look I will do everything I can to stop the flow but you will have to put up with it as we have some real problems with Jackie. I am worried she is coming apart!"

"Oh help me trouser, quickly, I am damaged. I have lost a button already and fear for my seams!" yelled a terrified Jackie.

"At least you're not drowning in some warm liquid!" moaned Ted.

"Shut up!" I hissed, 'we need to get ourselves out of this so you MUST focus."

I heard an irritated gurgle from Ted but no further complaint.

Feeling I had matters under control I fell back, literally, to trying to control our gentleman's movements, which were now totally unpredictable.

Suddenly a denim knee came thundering into my crotch and I doubled over in pain, certain I had split my zip.

"Are you OK Hugo?" I gasped as I straightened myself up.

"Fine," he groaned, 'I fink it was you whot took the worst of it, fanks."

"Quickly! Do something I think I have lost another button, help me," panicked Jackie.

"Oh hell, do you have any ideas Ted?" I enquired, exasperated.

I expected little intelligent comment from the flash Ted Bakers but to my surprise their thoughts, although angrily expressed, were worth a try.

"What about Mr Pink?" they said. "He is very quiet and is probably just hiding behind Jackie leaving her to take all the punishment."

"Brilliant idea Teds," I enthused as I raised the idea of help with Mr Pink.

"Nothing to do with me, old bean," he said in those strange lisping tones that all pink shirts use.

"Well it certainly will be if Jackie completely gives in and falls apart. You will have to defend yourself. Just think how easily you could lose all those delicate buttons and have your front ripped apart. Think of the damage and the pain and the shame when you end up in the outfitters A&E." I encouraged.

"OK I see your point Trouser, we could work together and defend our master," he said, now quite enthusiastically.

To my amazement I could see arms flailing and cuffs flapping. Jackie was making some strange noises like a Zulu warier and Mr Pink was using words that I never realised a quality shirt knew. Indeed some of the words were new to me.

Suddenly my thoughts were interrupted by a desperate growl from The Boss who I had completely forgotten.

"This is gettin urgent trouser, you twat, whatever you are doing out there is causing problems. I have now lost control of the front and I am not sure whether I will be able to hold the rear much longer.

The rumblins are gettin worse and if you don't do sommink soon I fear the worst. You must take control, trouser and do sommink."

I was totally bemused by his words, not concerning the problems, but the responsibility he was laying on me. He wanted me to be the leader. To be the one on whose survival every item of clothing suddenly relied. I panicked! I was not cut out for this task. It was obvious I had always been the liaison garment, the conduit between all others. I was in contact with all but, to control them, order them to follow my command was another matter. I was terrified I would let them all down.

"Come on trouser shift yerself, do something," The Boss yelled, followed by Teds who was back to their annoying selves.

"I must do it as everyone is relying on me!" I thought as I straightened my seams and sharpened my creases. "Here goes," I whispered to myself with a less than confident air.

"Right! Jackie and Mr Pink keep on the attack. I want to see those arms working and those lapels firm and aggressive."

"Will do sir," they both shouted breathlessly.

"Teds, you and I are going to work together and deliver the winning blow. We must attack with aggression. Are you ready Teds?"

"Yes," they said in a less than confident tone, clearly not sure what was actually required of them.

"We are going to combine our force and kick out with our left foot as hard as we can." Feeling Ted's right foot twitch in anticipation I yelled "No not that left foot the other left foot. We will then take our assailant by surprise."

I yelled, "Go!" and we launched our combined might at the shins of the opponent, forcing him to move back. This released Jackie and Mr Pink for a brief respite. I could hear their heavy breathing as they painfully checked their buttons and seams.

"Come on, let's keep going," screamed Teds now high on the adrenalin of battle.

It did not take us more than a moment to get into the rhythm of attack. Left then right then left, now somewhat higher, then lower. Eventually I had to restrain the Teds, fearing, in their enthusiasm, they would wear themselves out.

It was soon clear the battle was over and we all cheered. Our gentleman was now sober and none the worse, thanks to our efforts.

That night, as we lay in a heap on the bedroom floor, we all recounted our various exploits and congratulated each other. It was then that The Boss turned to me and with tears in his Y-front, said. "The day goes to you, Trouser, wivout yer leadership we would 'ave ended up a heap of torn rags, left to rot in the street, totally buggered"

"Rather than on the bedroom floor!" lisped Mr Pink, and we all laughed.

My modesty found it difficult to accept such praise and I turned to them and with a trembling voice said, "It was no thanks to me we won, it was all of you working as a team. I think it is time for a team hug don't you?"

From that day onward we all worked together at whatever tasks we were set, even Teds insisted on being part of the team whenever they could. I am quite sure our gentleman certainly noticed a difference.

One thing was true. There would be no further outings for us until a visit to the cleaners and possibly the A&E outfitters.

The Battle of the Grapes

One day, when our gentleman was resting at work, after a good lunch, I became aware of The Boss trying to attract my attention. Now at this time each day all is generally quiet which gives us clothing time to relax our weave and prepare ourselves for whatever happens in the latter part of the day and sometimes night. I was therefore somewhat irritated when The Boss disturbed my repast but it happened so rarely I realised it must be important. I therefore brought myself to focus on his wavelength. Not that we are connected in any way by wavelengths but it is a general expression that describes a connection between items of clothing.

The Boss expressed his concerns that warped my weave and twisted my stitches. He told me quite categorically that our gentleman was growing grapes up his bottom. I have never disbelieved The Boss and, knowing him to be short of the practical jokes skills, I was inclined to believe him but this was nothing I could understand or even begin to contemplate. My only advice was to throw it open for discussion at the full meeting of the wardrobe on this coming Saturday.

The Boss agreed to open the debate and, following his almost tearful oratory, every member of the wardrobe was stunned into silence. I tentatively progressed the proceedings by presenting the worst case scenario. I proposed our master had lost his mind and decided to grow grapes up his bottom as a horticultural project. I suggested that if this project was a success the next stage would be to grow a whole vegetable patch.

The consequences of this created such a hubbub in the wardrobe that The Boss found it difficult to restore order. I have to admit the Clark brothers disappointed me somewhat as, being remote from the consequences, they found the whole idea quite amusing. Jackie, bless her, tried to help by suggesting that she had heard the expression 'growing potatoes' in socks which rather quietened the disrespectful brothers. Mr Pink, being a most sensible shirt, noted that our gentleman had been drinking a lot of red wine recently and it may be that a pip from the wine grape had lodged itself in his bottom and grown there. The Boss expanded his concerns by niggling that if the project grew the whole shape of the wardrobe would change as he would be in no position to contain such a development. He thought he may even be replaced by some sort of horticultural underwear.

To my surprise it was the Sneakers who progressed the matter by summarising the need to take some action. They laid it open to the full meeting to make some decision for action. There were many mumblings but no one seemed to have an answer. Suddenly The Boss, who is generally known for his calm clear thinking, yelled irritably for silence. In a tantrum like rhetoric he yelled that if nobody else could come up with an idea he would take the initiative and put himself in danger by squeezing the offending fruits and destroying them. This seemed to obtain support from most of the clothing as it was hoped that if the project succeeded our gentleman would stop such a foolish carry on and take up a more sensible mode of hobby.

It was agreed then and The Boss was left to choose the right moment to obliterate the fruity protrusions in a hope that it would be the end of the matter. It was thus that one day during a relaxing lunch The Boss summoned up all his energy and much of his courage and squeezed as hard as he could. Unfortunately the result was not as we had all hoped. It appeared that we had caused our master some considerable pain and his screams and clutches at The Boss caused much shame to us all.

The following day before work we took a detour to a doctor's surgery. This was a new experience for The Boss as we were unceremoniously dropped to our master's ankles in a far different way from the provocative manner we had experienced on other occasions. The Boss being more of a garment of the world kept mumbling about some sort of homosexual act but I was none the wiser. The man in the white coat peered at the bunch of grapes and prodded them as if he was about to purchase a bunch. He seemed extremely interested in the fruit and I was somewhat fearful of the outcome of such examination. We need not have worried however as we were soon fastened back into our rightful place and proceeded to go to work.

The failure of our operation was the key discussion point of the next wardrobe meeting. Gone were the witticisms of the previous meeting and there was a general air of concern. Suggestions emerged only to be struck down with genuine feeling. It was during one of these discussions that all hell broke loose and we had the most disgraceful occurrence of my known days. To this day I had no idea how it started as my first awareness of the issue was the Clark brothers kicking the Sneakers. I had heard the Sneakers threatening to resign the wardrobe but as there were no pleas for them to stay I thought they had retracted the idea, I was told later it was at this point the Clark brothers suggested it was a good idea for them to go. Clearly, as rivals for our gentleman's attention, they were never great friends but to sink to these depths in what was generally a well-mannered wardrobe was untenable. I thrust my leg in between them and boldly roared for silence. As the kickers calmed down I lectured them on their disgusting behaviour and warned that if anything like that occurred again they would all be dismissed from the wardrobe.

Now I knew that such an action was beyond my authority but I was fairly sure that most of the wardrobe did not. Clearly Jackie knew as she gently squeezed my zip in support, an action that generally sends me into total confusion.

Calm now having descended on the meeting the consideration of the issue was once more upon us. It was then that my dear Jackie came up with the most profound statement that 'no action' was the most worthwhile action. It was a bit too subtle for the Sneakers and one or two pairs of Marks and Sparks socks but the rest of us picked up on the idea immediately. 'Let's see what happens' was the final decision and clearly noted in the minutes. The meeting broke up with the behaviour of the day dissected by every group.

It was some days later that The Boss once again called me aside. I was worried that he was about to inform me that some other form of vegetable had appeared. A cucumber or lettuce even sped through my mind. The news however was good as the grapes had disappeared and I was pleased to report that they did not return.

Bicycle Ride

I have always considered myself a fairly active trouser, many have agreed with me, so when one day, after work I found myself not on the usual route to the pub I was not concerned. It was a nice sunny evening and my gentleman, I discovered, had decided to go for a cycle ride. I was still not worried. This was partly because I had no idea what a cycle ride was and how it would involve me. Jackie, of course, with her higher view on things giggled herself almost to a frenzy when she heard of the gentleman's ambition. She refused to advise me of my involvement and, despite my growling anxiety, she simply gurgled to a breathless silence. I assured myself there was still nothing to worry about.

My gentleman borrowed a bicycle contraption from a so called caring friend and carefully pushed it to a secluded area away from any audience. I am not easily frightened, and I certainly was not now, but the feeling of uncertainty and Jackie's chuckling did not help my confidence. I am not stupid enough to be unable to understand wheels as a means of getting about. My dilemma however, was that this array of tubes only seemed to have two wheels. There is also, from my point of view, the most important issue and that is where my gentleman will be sitting or, more importantly, where he will be placing me and what function I will have to perform. My seams were beginning to twitch with a little agitation at these concerns but they were stiff enough to reassure me I was not worried.

It soon became sadly clear that my gentleman's lack of skill in simply pushing the contraption was an indication of worse to come. At first he exploded into a tumble when he managed to catch his foot on a pedal and dive through the frame to the ground. I was now more than worried, more terrified, as I thought my knee had been torn. Fortunately there was no damage. If this was cycling, I feared for my safety.

Arriving at flat, straight ground my gentleman decided to attempt the seemingly easy acrobatic task of mounting the vehicle. Firstly, out of clear respect for my wellbeing, he tucked my leg bottoms into his socks, The Ted Bakers, of course. As always they were loud in their protestation of my extra intimacy but I had little concern for their feelings. I know I must have looked a dreadful sight and just hoped that none of my old chums from Saville Row would spy me. I knew I would be the laughing stock of the whole street if word got out. I need not have worried however, as this was hardly a place where a decent Saville Row suit would normally be taken. In my shame and, also somewhat relieved, I was certain I would be the only respectable suit in the area.

Straightening up, my gentleman took a sudden swing of his leg and his foot landed on the other side of the conveyance with an appearance of controlled animation, narrowly missing the saddle in the process. My experience of the manoeuvre was less than positive. I feared my seams were going to split but fortunately the superior weave and skill of my tailor held me together with the might of a strong denim. I suddenly felt myself moving forward as my gentleman, almost athletically, propelled us along a path chosen it seemed more by the vehicle than my master's control. Then he sat on the saddle!

Now a bicycle saddle is an odd shape and certainly not designed to be used by a carefully crafted quality suit. Jacky was alright, enjoying the breeze through her lapels with her pleats flying out behind her. I could hear her excited song as our speed increased and the wind caressed her pocket flaps. My situation however was quite the opposite. A gentleman's suit is designed specifically for a gentleman in a standing position, the side on which he dresses being carefully crafted as a result of attentive whisperings between the tailor and his customer. With a bicycle saddle the long protrusion at the front makes the positioning of my gentleman's manhood a tricky affair. With his legs pumping, this action leads to the switching of his equipment from one side to the other, on a regular basis. Without my careful adjustments I knew he could be in serious pain and cause possible lasting damage. This manoeuvre was made more difficult due to the subtle pocketing of the left leg to allow for the left hand side hang. The friction of this activity also led to a warming of the inner thighs and made me frightened of lasting damage to myself and my gentleman, caused by the constant rubbing.

I was not to worry for long however, as an unnoticed wooden log suddenly halted the contraption and pivoted my man over the handlebars into a hedge, causing serious damage to the front wheel. My master disentangled himself from the foliage and examined himself and, to my gratification, me for any sign of injury. Fortunately, he discovered no damage and switched his attention to the bicycle. I could feel the anger in his frame and suddenly grabbing the length of twisted metal, jettisoned it into the hedge that he had so recently occupied, leaving it to be collected and repaired at a later date.

My first thought was for Jackie as such a tumble could have torn any part of her. Upon inspection I reassured myself that she was fine, just a little crumpled and dispirited. I know it was churlish of me to think it but I was a little amused at her whining on the return journey about the way she had been manhandled and the fact that it was no way a Saville Row jacket should be treated. I just smiled at the remembrance of the happy noises I had heard only half an hour ago.

It was not long after this event we were joined in the wardrobe by a pair of black, tight fitting Lycra shorts. They were far too ostentatious for my liking but Jackie seemed to enjoy his company and so called witty repartee. I was not at all jealous of this fraternisation. I knew it would not come to anything as I was confident Jackie would certainly not go out with him. It seems he particularly enjoyed the manoeuvrings of the bicycle saddle as he was specially designed to manage a gentleman's encumbrances, flexible enough to flick the items from side to side. His only complaint was due to the revealing nature of his cut he was often manhandled, sometimes quite savagely, at the drinking sessions that always followed the exertions.

Jackie and I Separate

As a working trouser I was subjected to sweat more times than Jackie so inevitably I was sent to the cleaners more often. This was, in fact, an outing that I rather enjoyed, not being without Jackie you understand, but the invigoration was such that my weave stiffened and my whole cut felt like new. When eventually I returned to the wardrobe I always slid under Jackie on the hanger with a feeling of pride and excitement. I loved rubbing up against her once more with an aroused weave and stiffened seams.

It was on such an occasion that I slipped a little from the hanger, arriving on the floor and coming into contact with a pair of sneakers. I knew they were in the wardrobe of course but tried not to have contact with them and, quite honestly, did not value their company. This brushing together, however, was out of my control but I felt no enthusiasm for joining them in conversation. Regrettably, their sentiment was totally the opposite and after the usual pleasantries of a well-controlled wardrobe they delighted in informing me of certain occurrences they stated they had observed.

Now sneakers, by their very name, have a reputation for causing trouble in the wardrobe, sharing information with others that may or may not be true. Being such inadequate footwear they rarely venture into the outside world so they try to glorify their existence by stirring up untruths and upsetting any chosen victim they happen to brush up against in their allotted space. This was well known so I believed very little of their fiery whisperings regarding Jackie.

They hissed that every time I went to the cleaners Jackie went out with a denim trouser. I was somewhat shocked that they should concoct such an absurdity but I was certain they were wrong. I knew Jackie too well to believe she would have anything to do with such trash.

Whilst the idea remained in my mind the whole concept was beyond my belief. Against my better judgement I could not stop myself from listening to the sneakers who persisted with their insinuation. They railed that Jackie had confided in them how she found such a stiff seamed and starched trouser like me, so boring. They suggested Jackie would prefer the excitement of being with a rough pair of denims treating her with little respect other than as an exciting plaything.

I tried to think nothing of these jibes but it eked away at my linings and I just could not let it go. It was clearly not an issue I could discuss with her in the wardrobe with everyone listening and giggling, but I had to have a private conversation with her.

Not long after, when I was trying to work a plan where we would be alone together we found ourselves thrown on the floor after one of my gentlemen's evening of drinking.

We shared the usual discussions about the evening's activity as I was nervous to broach such a delicate subject immediately. I felt however, it had to be done to satisfy my mind, so I stiffened my creases and confronted my dear Jacket with the accusations, expecting an immediate denial of such activity. I was therefore, totally flabbergasted when she responded, "So why shouldn't I go out with whoever I want," she hissed, in such an aggressive manner I was unable to speak at first. I was so devastated with her words that my seams wilted and my creases softened. I pleaded with her that we were made together, of the same cloth, and we could not be separated. Her sneered response wilted my zip and my waistband drooped in emotional turmoil.

"Ok," she said, "we are made of the same cloth but that does not make us lovers, we are not Onesies you know. The closest we could get to a human understanding would be brother and sister. Surely you are not suggesting brother and sister should be lovers. If I want to have fun with a trouser of another cloth then I am quite entitled to do so! I have, and I enjoyed it every time."

My devastation was complete and it was not long before her cavorting with the denim was open knowledge. I thought it was just a midlife fling and it would quickly die out but soon we were moved to different hangers and she hung out with the denim.

Trousers, of course, do not have hearts but we have feelings and my life seemed to be at an end. I could feel no reason for existing or serving my gentleman. I was devastated, betrayed by a stupid jacket. My misery was complete.

After a while, to straighten my seams a little, I tried going out with a denim jacket just to spite Jackie. It was not the same and, I have to say, I learned a lot about the antics of such an outing that make me blush even now. One night out with a Pringle was much better but all she talked about was golf and had no enthusiasm for sensible conversation.

What sunk me into my final despair was an outing with a leather jacket. Now we all know that by their very nature leather jackets are tough, sometimes unruly but, if treated with respect, I believed can be good company. Our evening started off well with a few drinks in a biker's bar and Leather and I seemed to hit it off. My hell started when we wobbled out into the night air and mounted the passenger seat of a Harley. A wide seated vehicle at its best and with Leather squeezing me tight, I was out of control. We whizzed off and my crotch was swept back in the saddle grasping on to stop from falling off the back.

Leather was whooping with delight as we leaned over, frightening me that my knee would be ripped on the fast approaching road surface as we turned a corner at terrifying speed. We then spun to the other side and I found the other knee drifting to a tearing contact. A trouser of course is not capable of being sick and that is a human experience I am glad not to suffer but, once we eventually alighted, I was very much aware of my gentleman's buttocks being much tighter than I had ever experienced.

The Charity Shop

The wardrobe rumour machine had been active as usual and all the gossip was about me. The story was that as I was no longer with Jackie I was of little use to the gentleman. They said I had not been out for a long time and it was only a matter of time when I would be the subject of one of the master's clear outs, and ejected to the life beyond the wardrobe. I was, of course, concerned about a change in lifestyle but life in the wardrobe was becoming intolerable. I was still hanging about close to Jackie and to see her constantly caressing the scruffy denim, giggling, whispering and fondling his ostentatious seams made me angry. To myself I was quietly crying as I saw them go out together, leaving me on my own, in my misery.

I was relieved, in a way, when I found myself in a large plastic bag with a number of other clothes. I knew them all well as, of course, we had lounged together in the wardrobe for several years. Some of them were quite a bit older than me and rather worn. All had seen better days and I shuddered to think that the same applied to me. I had been out with many of the garments but to be honest I had little time for most of them as none were handmade and some looked rather cheap. I was certainly in no mood to fraternise with such trash.

I looked around and was disappointed that Jackie was not with us but I had to accept that she had found a new life and just hoped she was happy. I certainly had my doubts that a denim could make such a sophisticated jacket as my Jackie, happy but I had to accept it was her life to lead any way she wanted. I kept trying to remove such thoughts from my mind but when we have been through so much together it is difficult not to be sad about a broken relationship. My own life moved to unknown theatres with a hope that I would continue to act in a caring gentlemanly way.

Sometime later we were tipped out onto a rather dusty floor, with hundreds of other garments, and sorted into piles of similar orientation. I was somewhat disappointed to find myself jumbled with any sort of trouser. I felt that I should at least be separated from the more common trouser. I assumed my superior cut and cloth was obvious for everyone to see. I even found myself tumbled with the odd second hand denim but I quickly manoeuvred myself from its threatening presence.

After sorting, we were carefully hung on large racks to be sold to anyone who was prepared to pay the price which seemed uncommonly cheap to me. At this stage I was still naive enough to believe our purveyor would vet the purchaser of such a refined garment as myself and not allow any riffraff to corrupt my perfect cut. I was soon to be disappointed with such an ideal. This was a shock to me at first as I did not feel myself to be a common trouser to be hawked in the market place for every soul to paw over.

Being of strong character I soon set to and accepted the reality of my situation. I straightened myself and sharpened my creases. I pulled myself up and decided that such a superior garment as myself would soon be snapped up by a discerning well healed gentleman. My thoughts were strengthened when I heard the growl of a denim next to me urging me to budge up to give him more room to be viewed. I sneered at him and stiffened my hanger to ensure my rightful space. I was certain that with such common garments as these my days on display would be very short.

The first day the shop opened there was a surge of customers sifting through the racks eager to find a bargain. Many of my new comrades were soon snapped up and transported to fresh ownership, never to be seen again. At the end of the day my neighbour, the denim had received quite a mauling but unfortunately remained next to me. I however had not been touched, except to be pushed to one side by people trying to get to other clothes. It was a disappointing day but I was sure the next morning would soon see me in the hands of a new well-dressed gentleman.

As the lights went out I settled down to a quiet night amongst my new friends. I was sure we would find something in common that would help us to while away the long night hours. I was soon sadly disillusioned as 'common' was the operative word. They talked, oh boy, did they talk, but it was such inane drivel that I had little interest in the subjects and refused to participate on debates concerning the merits of their previous owners.

It was not long before the dreadful denim next to me spotted some pretty dresses on the rail opposite. I had noticed them before and tried to engage them in some polite conversation but with little effect as my efforts were simply met with inane tittering. The denim, I am sure, did not know the meaning of polite and the things he said to these lovely garments made me shudder with disgust. To my horror the dresses responded with enthusiasm and there were soon hoots and shoutings of the most obscene kind, it made my seams creak.

The next morning arrived at last and after a brief straightening we were again revealed to the public. There was extra room on the rails today so I had a more prominent position and was determined to present myself in a positive way. I removed the horrors of the night from my mind and removing my wrinkles straightened my seams and creases and showed my determination to make a positive contribution to any gentleman's wardrobe. I was unfortunately ignored again and forced to spend another dreadful night in this clothes asylum.

A month went by and still I had not been selected and, worse still neither had my denim tormenter. If I could I would have happily killed him, ripped his threads out and left his pockets bare on the ground. I knew such a thing would not be acceptable but it helped to keep me sane in those dismal nights of penance. My legs were wrinkling, my creases were sagging and I knew I could not take much more of it.

Another day, another depression and I settled myself to being shifted to and fro to make way for a sight of my colleagues. 'Choose me, choose me' I pleaded desperately to any gentleman that came near, but my begging went unheard. Most of my acquaintances had now gone and I was almost alone with the damned denim. When he finally went, at a cut down price I was pleased to see, I thought I would be overwhelmed with joy. However, to my amazement I missed him and my devastation and depression was complete. Alone, soon to be demoted to the rubbish tip, my creases warped with overwhelming depression and failure.

At my wits end, imagine my joy one day when an oldish gentleman removed me from my hanger and held me against himself to check for a fit. In times gone by I would have shouted, "You are too big for me," but I had to get away from this mess so I stretched myself out to assume the most perfect fit. My ruse worked and I found myself carefully folded and placed in a bag for protection. All of a sudden my pride returned, my wrinkles had gone and my creases straightened. I felt like a brand new trouser, ready to start my new life.

The New Gentleman

I was so excited as I hung up in the wardrobe. Lots of new friends and, at first glance, all reasonably respectable. I knew instantly I was going to like it here. A closer inspection and I saw a suit at which I respectfully nodded.

There is always a hierarchy in a wardrobe which we all knew must be adhered to at all times. Naturally, the head of the list is the suit. I had already spotted that he was not made of such quality material as me but he was a suit and I was simply a trouser now. I threw an admiring glance at the jacket but knew that such approaches would certainly be out of order.

I felt however that being of a high quality cut and good material I fell easily in line as the second most important person in the wardrobe. My breeding was quickly recognised and most accepted the new structure. All the young slacks treated me with respect although there was a young chino who I could tell did not quite like the new set up. A quiet word from the suit soon put him in his place. I glanced down at the shoes, after all they were going to be my close companions. I felt a slight pain of horror as I saw a number of trainers who, in terms of the hierarchy, fall to the lowest category. There were however a pair of black and a pair of brown leather shoes and I immediately assumed they would be my companions. I was a somewhat nervous about the brown shoes as I had discovered it was a modern practice to wear brown shoes with a dark trouser. I was totally against the idea being of the more conventional persuasion but I accepted that I had to move with the times. Anything was better than a close relationship with a pair of trainers.

My excitement grew as, on my first morning, I was ceremoniously removed from my hanger, matched with a clean, but in my view rather common shirt and was hauled on my gentleman with pride. I was slightly nervous about the underpants as they were of the cheap variety and seemed to achieve very little in the way of support for my new gentleman. I was also not quite sure of the amount of protection they would afford me in the more intimate areas. None the less I was going out and excited to learn of my gentleman's habits and ways of dealing with the world.

We walked smartly down the street, stretching myself to make the fit I had feared to be too tight, smiled at the black shoes, my new intimate friend, and enjoyed the journey.

A trouser, as I am sure you know, cannot tell the time because we have no need to. A jacket, of course, is in a different position, often being close to a wrist watch or at least within sight of a clock. Anyway, I had a feeling we were somewhat late for work on my first morning with my new gentleman. I had no problem with this and considered my gentleman had one of those special jobs that did not require him to be early. I was still somewhat surprised however when we entered a building that was obviously a public house. Now my aforementioned inability to tell the time caused me to wonder somewhat as it seemed quite early to enter such an establishment. Indeed, I was sure my previous gentleman, despite his sometimes extended occupation of such an establishment, would not commence his imbibings at such an early time.

After an hour or two I decided my gentleman was on holiday and so was spending his day in relaxing company, although I was not aware of any such company. I was proud that I had been selected for such an occasion. The time dragged on and despite a few trips to the toilet nothing seemed to happen.

The day flowed monotonously onward and the toilet visits became more frequent. It was soon that my worst fears had been realised and my companion underpants failed in their task to hold back the ever increasing dribble. It was thus that I was ashamed of the spreading wet patch that was clearly visible to all.

We spent the whole day there and, by the end of it, our homeward journey was somewhat ragged. Indeed, it was all I could do to propel my master's legs in the right direction. Upon arrival, after a few bendings to pick up dropped front door keys, we staggered up the stairs to bed. At this stage we suffered the inevitable problem of separating man from trouser without falling over. I was determined to make this task easy and once unfastened, my waist slipped to the gentleman's ankles with ease. This was where the problem started as he had not taken care to remove his shoes. My legs could not slide over the shoes and so my gentleman's legs were tied together. He bent down to remove the items that were now becoming offensive and the sudden rush of blood or alcohol to his head made him topple over, gently arriving on the carpet with a violent curse followed by a girlish giggle. The shoes refused to budge despite my curses and my legs were wedged tightly round their tops. My master's solution to this was to lie on his back with his feet in the air trying to release my legs from the shoes so he could dispel the offending items. Now had it been the Clark brothers their superior crafting would have made it a simple task but these rather cheap items of footwear did not have the wit to respond to the problem. I was frustrated and terrified because I was sure my seams would burst and my man seemed to have no ability left in his hands to enable him to slide my legs up to his waist. He was like a man possessed, ripping at me without a care of the damage he could do. Suddenly, with our joint effort, my legs slipped back and the shoes, suddenly released, flew across the room in an excited escape to freedom. It was now easy for me to be removed from my gentleman and we both lay on the floor in a crumpled heap, to spend the night in shame and discomfort. Well it was for me, but I believe my master had little interest in such stuff.

The next morning I was wrinkled and crumpled but was looking forward to a day resting in the wardrobe. I soon realised this was not to be, as I was yanked into place on my master's person and found myself off to the pub again. This was the procedure every day. I was almost worn out and was afraid that such rough treatment would cause permanent damage.

The Wardrobe

On the odd occasion I made it to the wardrobe I knew I was losing control of my status because I was never there. My position as number two had been usurped by the Chino and I discovered I received little respect from the other garments. The suit had called me to one side and suggested I pulled myself together and try to look less shabby. I know I should not have said it but in my frazzled state I simply lost control. I screamed at him that he was just a 'Marks and Spencer' suit who had no idea how a gentleman's suit should behave and he had no right to talk to me like that. My behaviour became the subject of the next wardrobe meeting and I was given a first warning.

On one of the few days I was in the wardrobe I mistakenly slipped off the hanger and fell to the bottom. Before I could gather myself I was pounced on by several trainers. They started trampling me and kicking me around until I found myself crumpled in a corner trying to defend myself. It was then that a strong pair of brown moccasins sprang to my rescue and shoed the trainers off. He checked for any injuries but told me not to worry as the trainers were just a bunch of overpaid sports attire that had no sense of responsibility. He told me about the old days before trainers became fashion wear. When they were far less well paid and were simply athletic foot attire known as plimsolls.

Despite the help from the moccasin, when I eventually found myself back on a hanger all my confidence had evaporated. I was crumpled on an end looking frighteningly out for any denim or other aggressive attire that might challenge me. I was coming apart and was desperately in need of a garment psychiatrist but there was no such opportunity. I spent the nights crying for Jackie and longing for the soft caresses of The Boss. My life as a well-made garment was nearing an end and I began to whimper that my seams would droop open and my life end. I was already creased all over and there was no sign of my previous proud vertical straight creases.

I was totally exposed and had no jacket under which to hide, no one would speak to me and eventually I found, on the suit's instruction, I was sent to Coventry and even the trainers refused to talk to me. I was ostracised from the whole wardrobe.

Life was intolerable I had no companions and I was mal-treated during the day suffering long days of arduous labour with little or no respite. I was in serious danger of totally coming apart.

Whilst in this state I hardly heard a rough croaking voice say "Trouser up old bean, life is not that bad. I know this is a fairly common wardrobe inhabited by cheap garments but that is all the more reason why us well made gentleman's attire must keep a stiff seam and show this trash that we are a class above them."

I gathered my senses and examined the source of the voice. It was clearly a well-made blazer but had certainly seen better days. Not all the buttons were present and the lapels were a trifle limp. There were also some rather vivid stains down the front, partly, I surmised of red wine and unidentifiable meals that a gentleman had once enjoyed.

"Things are not as bad as they seem," he growled. "I am more than pleased to make your acquaintance and will happily have a word with the suit to ensure this poor behaviour towards you will not continue. I would be pleased to go out with you but I do not think it would improve the situation as these common garments are such bigots," he croaked.

"I suspect I can help in another way though. You probably did not notice in your miserable state, but at the other end of the rail is a young lightweight jacket that has been checking you out. These are things I notice in my mature years and I think there is a serious interest there which could raise your spirits. I have in fact taken the liberty of arranging for the two of you to go out together. Nothing special you understand but I think it would do you good."

I immediately flushed with embarrassment as despite one or two dabblings I had not been out with anyone since Jackie. I had lost all my confidence and felt terrified at such an outing with a strange jacket.

Bernard the Blazer introduced me to Lucy the lightweight before we went out just to help me with my shyness. I have to say the outing was not as bad as I had expected. Lucy was a friendly garment, in fact I felt a little too friendly for a first outing. She was quite chatty and kept me amused although she was a lightweight and therefore had little in the way of good conversation and her constant giggling soon became a source of annoyance to me.

I appreciated the gesture by my friendly blazer but whilst we remained polite it was never going to be a long term relationship but it did serve to brighten me up.

The Barmaid

Some days however were more tolerable than others. As I have said before, a trouser does not have a specific sex but being rather close to a gentleman's equipment I could not help pick up on some of the sensations projected from such items. It was thus that I spotted a rather attractive blouse the other side of the bar. In my view the blouse was somewhat too small for its wearer as it revealed more of a pair of rather large breasts than I felt was necessary. I followed my gentleman's thoughts as I watched the blouse caress the special features as the lady performed her duties to the delight of most of the customers. My gentleman, once again, spending all day in the same position, seemed to get to know the lady well so much so that the amount of drink consumed appeared to be less than usual.

When it was time to go home I found myself accompanied by a rather attractive pair of olive green tights, stretched prettily over a number of curves. We found our way strolling along the canal and under a bridge we stopped and pressed together.

Now sex is rather a mystery to me as I have often thought about it but failed to arrive at any clear understanding following my master's undertakings. I wondered if what I did with Lucy was sex. I certainly enjoyed it and she seemed to know what she was doing. The best sex was always with Jackie as her caresses used to cover my seams and then melt to my zip which instantly stiffened to her soft movements. This I can contrast with my one outing with the leather jacket whose crazy wild rubbings took me some time from which to recover.

My first observation of my gentleman's sexual activity was the loud slurping noises that seemed to be coming from his mouth. It was similar to this gentleman eating, which he rather enjoyed, but somewhat more frantic. The next move occurred when my gentleman popped out the large breasts and was certainly eating them, resulting in the barmaid releasing large gusts of what appeared to be ecstasy.

My gentleman's arousal was soon stretching my zip to its very limits. It was thus that I was gratefully relieved when a female hand loosened my waist and undid my zip.

What happened next caused my involvement in the sexual exchange to cease and be replaced by more urgent matters. I sunk rapidly to the ground and to be honest was eager to distance myself from the excited activity with my gentleman and the young barmaid. I certainly did not wish to go through the horror experienced on my new gentleman's first drunken night. The rather weak minded trainers were happy to release me from my gentleman's legs and I found myself totally detached. As I was released from the current thrustings I suddenly realised I was slipping towards the water. Without arms it is difficult to hang onto the bank. My legs however clasped as firmly as I could to a clump of grass but as my struggles simply made me slip further my waistband dipped into the watery mud and I glided silently into the river. The current soon caught me and I started floating down the stream separated from my gentleman, probably for ever.

Life with a Tramp

At first I luxuriated in the cool water running through my being, washing away the soil of my previous existence. I was slowly cruising through the water calmly floating to who knows where but just pleased to be free of my previous master.

After a while it became cold, however, as my seams and every part of me became soaked. I was beginning to sink and had fears of disappearing into the depths to disintegrate into a watery grave. After a while I realised I had stopped moving and was wedged near the bank in a muddy ooze. I then became aware of various proddings of my seams by a stick manoeuvred from the bank. At the end of the stick was a somewhat dishevelled man who was clearly attempting to rescue me. Although a little apprehensive concerning my rescuer and his purpose I was keen to be extracted from the water. I therefore wove my legs round the stick in an attempt to make it easy for my saviour to extract me from the turgid slime. It seemed however that he was not adept at such a task and I feared a further launch into the stream and landing somewhere, abandoned and left to rot. It seemed though that this gentleman's desire to save me was so strong that he abandoned the stick and staggered into the mud bending down to extract me. Unfortunately this act of bending had some sort of negative affect on his equilibrium and he plunged head first into the flowing water. I reacted quickly, now concerned about our joint safety. I wrapped my legs round his arms steadying him and enabling him to return to the vertical. He managed to drag us both to the bank and enjoyed a welcomingly draining of water.

I had expected to be returned to a dry place and cleaned and pressed ready for whatever duties were required of me. This however, was not the case as after such exercise my saviour simply laid where he was and slept. It was not until the morning sun shed its dappled light in his face that he woke and started to inspect me. I was clearly not at my best as the mud had hardened into a grey covering that concealed all my best seams and stitching. I feared that seeing me in such a state he would return me to my watery grave. He fortunately saw beyond my filth and shaking the worst off me smiled admiringly at my noble weave. I felt proud and was convinced my life was to take a turn for the better. I was shocked though as his existing trouser was ripped from his body and tossed carelessly into the water. A pang of sorrow overcame me as I saw the poor dilapidated garment fall limply into the water and float weakly through the ripples, clearly on its way to end its days rotting its already weak seams.

My thoughts were soon awakened when I found myself being hauled onto my new master's body without cleaning or support from any type of undergarment. Fortunately the dowsing of the stream had cleansed the worst of my saviour's filth but the experience was not pleasant.

My new gentleman who retrieved me from the river bank was certainly no gentleman, more a tramp, a hobo or at best a gentleman of the road. I walked or rather he walked all day in the dusty dirty paths of suburbia. It was hot and relentless toil for a trouser that was made for comfort. I was designed for a snug fit but not too snug to chafe. My new owner was certainly not designed for snug as my crotch hung down a long way from its intended position and chafed continuously. The scrawny legs caused friction to warm my legs to an unbearable degree, such that I feared my seams wearing even more than they had already.

Eventually we settled in a filthy house littered with no more than flea ridden sleeping bags and the strange smell of urine and various types of smoking odour. It seemed no sooner had we arrived than I was roughly removed and rolled into a ball to form the shape of a pillow. My guardian's greasy head settled itself onto my bulked elegance and after a little rearrangement of my form, settled into a still slumber. It was not long before the saliva found its way from his mouth and soaked my cloth with its foul smelling dampness. I had been pleased that this current location appeared at least dry, despite the wild creatures inhabiting the nightly hunting forays, but this was not to be. My fine being was slowly soaking up the moisture and distributing it further through my seams.

So my new life consisted of a saliva filled night followed by a day of untold grime. Not only was I used as my skinny, smelly friend's lower covering but I also functioned as a cleaning cloth. When my saviour felt that his hands were dirty, and in my opinion that was always, he used me as a rag to clean the worst of whatever filth it was from his already engrained digits. I did my best to shake off what I could but there was no disguising the fact that I was becoming grubbier by the day. At times I was even used as a handkerchief but mostly such activity was performed by a rapid outpouring to the ground. Sometimes however the strings of slime still attached were wiped by hand and then deposited on my legs. I was certain there was no chance of a clean. I was so dispirited at times that I felt like ripping my seams and tearing every piece of thread from my cloth just to end my misery.

One night, accepting my lot and settling to another damp night I was suddenly interrupted by a hard yanking from behind. I was scrunched up and found myself stuffed in a bag and, moving rapidly to who knows where, left my erstwhile guardian with his head flat on the floor but peaceful in his dim witted slumber, drenching the dust laden floor with his liquid outpourings

Life with a Female

My future was not so certain as I soon found myself in what I believed to be a bus shelter fulfilling the same function as previously, a pillow. Trying to assess my situation I felt there was something very different about my new owner but I could not work out the full picture. Being in a bag did not make it easy to form a view of my new world but that was something that I had known before with my first gentleman. The fact that I was in a bag with other clothes was an improvement and I sensed, whilst not smelling of fabric conditioner there was a slightly more bearable, almost pleasant, pungency about my new comrades. I was aware that there was no such thing as wardrobe etiquette but I settled for the rest of the night with a comfort that I was sure I would enjoy in my new life.

The morning snapped upon me very quickly as I was hauled out of the now slightly fetid bag, releasing odours from the engrained clothing that had been absorbed from a proximity to my owner, the heat having stimulated the dried bodily oozings. I was still not sure what it was that was different about this life but there was something vaguely familiar. I was shaken and admired turned round several times and held up for examination in the now strengthening sunlight. I tried hard to look my best straightening my seams and stretching my wrinkles but I regret my recent treatment had aged me severely.

To my great delight I was soon dunked in a bowl of warm soapy water and scrubbed with a firmness that I felt was a little over enthusiastic at first. However, as the infestations and grime of my recent ownership seeped from me, my mood brightened. I was soon almost clean and found myself on a washing line dancing in the wind. I was a bit stiff at first with no experience of such an exercise but after a few twists I got the hang of it. I tossed my legs out as the wind caught me, kicking with joy at the freedom of my drying. It was not long before I was crossing my legs and swirling and turning like a pair of dancing tights. I was full of energy and as the wind died for a moment I hung limp to gain more energy for the next jig. After a time I managed to shift near a pink trouser and we danced together, sometimes entwined and then spin apart, in a whirl of happiness just like a couple of young knickerbockers. This was such fun I was sure I had the best owner ever. My joy, however, was not to last.

Once totally dry and fully invigorated I was introduced to my new task. As one leg and then another was slipped into me, my mood was bright as I was hauled to a well-fitting waist and fastened. Suddenly, as my crotch touched something with which I was not wholly familiar the lurid memories of my early master's philanderings came flooding back to me. I fearfully realised I was now owned by a woman!

This was wrong, it could not be, I screamed as my panic welled up inside me. I was not made for a woman as I did not have the right cut to fit the female shape and the threat to my seams was already causing discomfort. Surely the lady had made a terrible mistake and, realising this, would quickly return me to my old master with the appropriate apologies. As a gentleman's trouser I tried to avoid noticing the odour, but with nothing between me and flesh it was difficult to avoid a feeling of suffocating nausea as my lady paraded me through the streets.

My life became a nightmare as I was worn both day and night, never having an opportunity to ease my weave. I needed to breathe! I needed to be cleaned and breathe the air of a little freedom. It was hell but there was nothing I could do. I tried to split a seam hoping to be discarded but I was too well made and anyway I couldn't bring myself to do it. As the days teetered by, my misery increased with each horrific experience. I discovered that a female has little use for a zip unlike a gentleman. I felt my zip teeth starting to grow rusty and, worse still, I was forever being hauled up and down. I was frightened I would tear or lose my shape completely. As it was I could feel my weave loosening in certain places and my fear for certain seams in the damper places was driving me mad. I could feel my colour fading and the accumulated stains of constant wear were making me unrecognisable as a former (a matter which I recognised I had to come to terms with) gentleman's trouser.

I know it was no way for a gentleman's trouser to behave but I could not stand this unusual life any longer. There was a momentum to it that just did not fit in with my understanding of proper behaviour. I resolved to make my mistress's (a frightful word) life so uncomfortable that she would discard me. I knew I was taking a risk as I could end up in the incinerator and suffer an unpleasant end. I felt however my mistress was a kind soul and would simply dispose of me, not in hate, but an understanding of incompatibility. I started to make her itch, both back and front making it uncomfortable for her. I knew it was working as the continuous scratching was wearing me out. Indeed, I was fearful of being worn to holes but her scratching was both gentle and surreptitious. I sensed also that she was wearing a soreness in herself so needed to treated me with care so as not to make her problem worse.

Overseas Aid

It was not long before my wishes had come true. As I was deposited in a container marked 'overseas aid' I knew another stage in my life was about to unfold. Soon I found myself in a bag ready to be shipped to some foreign part. My faith in my mistress had been correct and I was sorry to be parted from her but we both knew we were totally incompatible.

I was soon tipped into a large container and thrown together with a vast heap of various garments. It rapidly became apparent that we were underway as the motion of the boat rocked us from side to side. I looked around at my assorted companions and felt the same apprehension I could feel from them all. We had no idea where we were going or what would happen to us when we got there. Nobody ever bothered to brief a load of old clothes. There were rumours of course, and one 'know it all' Pringle jumper, was quite insistent we were being recycled into some posh new clothes for gentry. This idea greatly heartened me but I knew the reality could be nothing like that. There was also the anguish about what garment I would become. The thought of ending up as some female attire made me feel giddy and I immediately dismissed the idea. There was no wardrobe procedure here so the opportunity for a well organised structured debate was impossible. The crying and weeping, shouting with anguish or just moaning with despair was intolerable. I just lay there ready to face whatever would come my way and tried to demonstrate my superior breeding.

Whilst I was ruminating on the various possibilities I noticed a rather nice looking pink jacket over the other side of our joint accommodation. Like us all, she looked rather worn but I could see that once she was a very smart and attractive piece of clothing. Using the motion of the ship I gradually edged towards her hoping to engage her in conversation and make the journey a little more pleasant for both of us. I was halfway to my destination when I was shocked to see a couple of denims roll straight on her. This was totally unacceptable behaviour and I could see she was becoming frightened of their proximity. Being a gentleman's trouser I resolved to immediately confront these ruffians and rescue the poor female. My chivalrous mission set, I hastened my attempt to get near her. I was not quite sure what I would do when I arrived, as denims can be quite vicious when aroused, but my mind was set in rescuing the damsel. Suddenly, from nowhere, a rather elderly but smart pair of cavalry twills appeared. He leapt on both denims rolling them to one side in a mighty movement of skilled confrontation that had clearly been well practiced in a lifetime of combat training. By this time I had arrived on the scene and, after checking the jacket was unharmed, I fell to congratulating the cavalry twills and expressing my admiration of his skills. Being the well put together gentleman's trouser that he was he dismissed my praises and looked to the jacket. We three soon became close friends and recounted stories of our past life making the long journey pass quickly. On arrival at a dusty, hot and malodorous part of the world we were separated and sorted again and after a tearful goodbye we never saw each other again.

Washing

We were left in a dirty, dusty and disorganised shed with nobody taking any notice of us. As I have said before a trouser does not have any idea of time but I knew we were suffering badly in such dreadful conditions. Many of my fellow inmates were oozing the fluid excreted from their previous owners and despite the potpourri of bad smells their seams were beginning to rot in the damp fetid enclosure.

The days dragged on with nothing happening to us and no human contact. It was the first time I had felt the need for human company. It surprised me as I had always considered myself a strong willed trouser not needing anybody. Despite the dubious companionship of a multitude of disintegrating garments my loneliness was beginning to overcome me.

One day when I was about to come apart, I found myself removed from my entombment and placed in a receptacle with an assortment of dirty washing all as desperately miserable as myself.

None of us really wanted to talk, all being too exhausted and worn to engage in any worthwhile conversation. I did however manage a brief introduction to a small shirt that I could see had been quite smart at one time but was now as worn and stained as us all. She was, however, able to tell me that we were going for our annual clean. This brightened my hopes but they were also dampened by her secret revelation. She had undergone this ritual several times and survived to be used again but she whispered to me that not everyone returned. The ordeal was sometimes too much for them and they simply fell apart, to be discarded to who knows where.

We were thrown together ready for the ordeal and a plan started to evolve. If I could mingle with other gentlemen's clothes I would escape any possible female entrapment like I had experienced before. It was a risk, of course, as I could end up in a worse situation. I could also be rejected by my new owner or worse still be attacked by a bunch of half crazed denims. After much reflection whilst huddling up to my new friend, the pretty shirt, I decided that nothing could be worse than my current situation so I waited for the right opportunity.

We were days waiting for something to happen and during that time I got to know Sally (the shirt) quite well. This gathering intimacy weakened my resolve somewhat as I had hoped that one day we might go out together. Such an ambition however was dashed when on one cold night, as we moved closer together for comfort, she confided in me. Her fear was that she had little hope of returning from the wash. She whispered that one or two of her seams were tearing and one armpit was almost rotted away. She had several buttons missing and believed her material was so thin she would simply fall apart.

We enjoyed a long night of clothing intimacy which, despite being created as a gentleman's trouser and groomed not to take advantage of such a situation, I convinced myself that I was giving her a final pleasure that she deeply deserved. I was certainly aware that her desire to bond gave her a lust for pleasure that I would have found difficult to resist. Our night flowed through waves of joint appreciation of each other's special treasures taking it in turns to enjoy the intimacy of coupling. Finally we rested and whilst she slept I wept at her pathetic state. However I did understand she was worn out and was happy to end her days in a washing machine clean and bright ready for her maker. I hoped she would go painlessly with a glowing memory of our night together.

Selection

The pleasant memory of my cleansing I considered was my baptism. I had at last rejected the arrogance of my past and accepted my fate with a belief that my creator, Gieves and Hawkes, had made me what I am. They had given me a sense of independence and strength of character to deal with whatever should happen to me. My new belief in myself and my creator left me with a deep purpose in my declining years. My task as I saw it was to try to look after other garments and do my best to console them. I should also do my best to keep my faith in my maker and perform my role in whatever way my path led.

I spent what appeared to be a long time in another shed with a variety of clothes. They had all been washed and I sensed had a more positive outlook on life. My new belief convinced me of my aim to befriend them all and help them wherever I could. Even the denims, after wrestling with my inbred feelings, I forced myself to try to help. My administrations were, as I feared, rejected but the more abuse I received from them the more determined I was to convert them into the ways of my maker.

My efforts were certainly straining me so when we were released into the light and carefully laid on the ground I felt immediately rejuvenated. I expected to be examined with the same behaviour I had experienced in the charity shop. Our potential owners however were somewhat different. They were mostly bare-chested and wore a variety of 'below the waist' clothing that did not appear to differentiate male from female. In fact in my position, lying on the ground, I became well aware that they had not been introduced to the likes of Hugo Boss or even a Marks and Spencer under-short! My old self would have yelped in horror at such views of a person's accoutrements and there was a momentary shudder of my stitching to imagine such intimacy with them. My new belief and understanding however, whilst tested, stood firm as I considered all my potential buyers as equals.

I was examined by all types of methods. I was pulled to test my strength, I was bitten and smelled and held up to the light but, to my surprise, I was never actually tried on. Once tested, I was then held tightly in one hand, while the other was used to emphasise the composition of the bargaining process. Sometimes I was even grabbed by a fellow citizen trying to wrench it from the bargainer's hand. The shouting seemed an important part of the debate but there was little interest in my wellbeing and, despite my new gentle demeanour, the strain on my stitching was almost more than I could bear.

Eventually an agreement was reached and only then, in front of all, was I hauled onto my comrade's body. This new description was my first test of the word and I decided I felt quite comfortable with the idea. I use this description now as I believe that everything is made equal and so there are no such things as owners or masters.

Now when I say my comrade hauled me on I expect dear reader you are visualising a perfect fitting garment caressing my new friends body to show it to perfection. I regret however this was far from the case. I was totally the wrong size. Without being unpleasant the man was very tall and skinny which was not my designed position. My first and reasonable thought was that I would be rejected and thrown back on the pile to be renegotiated to another more fitting purchaser. This however was not the case as my comrade grabbed hold of my waist rather roughly and hauled me up as far as my seams would allow. This, in fact, meant my waist band was rather nearer his nipples than his waist. The sudden lift caught me by surprise as I had no time to adjust and thus my seams split his two pear shaped balls into different halves of my legs and my rear seam disappeared into an extremely unpleasant crevice. A glance down at my legs and, fearing the worst, saw them dangling midway up his shins. In my view and I assumed in everyone else's view we looked ridiculous. This however appeared not to be the case as everyone encircled us prodding and poking and nodding their heads in approval. Suddenly they all took one step back and in unison clapped their hands in gleeful delight.

My comrade and I walked steadily along the dusty ground for a long time in the hot sun. I momentarily surfed back to my days long ago with the companionship of The Boss, Jackie and Mr Pink and thought how much they would enjoy such an outing on a warm summer's day in England. Unfortunately, this was not quite the same as The Boss was not with me to support me in my duties of gathering perspiration and holding it in my seams to avoid unsightly stains. In fact the threat of bad odour was also a problem in which my new comrade appeared to have little interest. As the progress continued I tried to gradually lower my waistband to its rightful position on his waist. The problem however was that having succeeded in this complex manoeuvre my crotch was now about knee level. Although a little uncomfortable and probably looking stupid I found I was able to swing my crotch from side to side thus making it easier for my friend to walk. This is what I assumed but it appeared my comrade was not as settled with the hang. He thus hauled my waist again but this time I was somewhat more prepared and so managed to squeeze the pears together to make a more comfortable lie and a more seemly bulge.

Feeling more settled with this array I suddenly found myself screaming with pain as a length of rough cord was wound round my band and pulled tight. I assumed it was to maintain the position below my friend's nipples. The pain was excruciating as it cut off most of the circulation to my upper weave the eventual consequences of which were too dire to imagine. Fortunately my comrade had extended his chest for this binding so upon relaxing the circulation returned and my pain subsided. The inevitable consequence though was for the waist to slowly shimmy down his body and restrict his knee action.

I was pleased that before any further strangulation of my cloth was undertaken we appeared to have arrived at our village. All the villagers undertook the same ritual as I had witnessed at the sale. All applauded except one rather young but pretty girl who I assumed with her obvious intimacy with my comrade was his daughter. Certain activities I witnessed later did not confirm this assumption indeed my doubts were somewhat strong. She spent some time looking at me pulling me up and sliding me down her man until she arrived at a view with which she seemed comfortable and indeed felt comfortable to me. She then grabbed my waist band and started to twist it round and round until it held firm at her man's waist. This was to no benefit for me as she stood back, admired her handy work, and walked away with my tearful screams of agony having no effect on her. Fortunately as the heat worked on me I was able to adjust things in a way that eased the tight wrinkles and softened my stretch marks. By the end of the day I was relaxed again and enjoying the admiring looks of both people and garments. An experience I had not had for many years.

Cut Offs

I was getting used to my life in the village. I was, I soon discovered, the trouser of the headman and as such, I held a rank of seniority amongst the other garments. We did not have the luxury of a wardrobe but often congregated in a special place in a hut or even sometimes in a selected heap outside the hut. Many people do not know that a trouser is multilingual but as such a superior garment I soon got to know all the others. Their manners were poor in comparison with the comrades of my youth but I did not find them difficult to befriend. It was not long before I was treated with the respect that my position demanded that of being the only long trouser of the village. As usual the few cut down denims I encountered were more aggressive than the rest. I had seen them worn by various senior members of the tribe, cut short and tight to their master's crotch with their pockets exposed. I could see they provided no support whatsoever and often allowed their owners genitals to drop below the sheltered level, forcing full exposure to the African sun. Not only this, but I was aware the young teenage females of the tribe were forever peering at the gentleman's crotch. Their hope to benefit from a peek at the gentleman's accoutrements believing they were entitled to such views. This they believed it enabled them to assess the man's ability to support them and produce fine sons. Their giggles revealed the hope of the shining pleasure such men might also gift them.

The denims still knew their place and despite their hard bitten stance they, like all of us, had a vast experience of life and knew the order of things. I knew my comrade was proud of me as, when in front of others, he would squat and brush my legs as if stroking a dog. When we crouched with other men in our conference circle I was aware that I was the only trouser that was capable of holding my master's equipment in control, even in a serious crouch position. His tool was of a noble generous size in comparison with the rest of him but my cloth was flexible enough now to accommodate such proportions. When I looked around the circle and saw the other gentleman's various bits sagging out through holes in the trousers or cut downs I was proud of my skills and felt my comrade was also pleased that a superior garment like me signalled the senior position in which he was held.

I soon became used to the fact that my master did not wear undershorts but accepted that this was the normal procedure. I was old now and rather than creases I had wrinkles cascading out in all directions from the main horizontal stretching. I was not too worried as I knew all of us garments were old and had come from other walks of life so we suffered the same problems. This was certainly no home for the elderly as I had hoped for in England but I was content.

The problem with continually squatting and kneeling is that it puts a great deal of pressure on the knees. I had always tried to manoeuvre myself in a way that eased the treacherous damage that could be inflicted on my knees. I relieved the weave in that particular section but I was always aware of the problem of wear and tear. There was nothing I could do and at every squat I feared the worst.

Inevitably the worst happened and as my comrade bent his knees at the head of the circle one day my right knee tore straight across the front, exposing my master's leg. Well, I thought positively, at least I will have a break now and have a visit to the tailors for an invisible mending. My negative thought was that I had never seen any garment that had been invisibly mended so their invisible mending was either very good or did not happen.

That night my fears were strengthened as I lay in the usual place with no attention whatsoever. I braced myself for a stitching the next day and hoped that such an operation would be well undertaken with the least pain and the tidiest of repairs. A strong over-sew would suffice and allow me to keep everything under control.

Several days passed and still nothing happened, other than the chief's continual usage of my being. I was beginning to feel weak with the flapping of my knee and the stretching of the damage.

Then, a few days later, the worst imaginable happened, my left knee split and I was now exposed on both sides. I screamed at this, hoping someone would notice my predicament but with none of my old type of friends such as socks, shoes and shirts I had no one to help. That night I lay in abject misery moaning at my dreadful state, hoping someone would come and sort me out.

Finally my pleadings were answered and I was picked up by one of the young females I had spotted before and carefully examined. She was giggling a little and I became very nervous when she handed me to other girls of similar age who pulled and stretched me in ways I had never experienced and with which I was not comfortable. Suddenly, they started tearing at my knees and, despite my screams, which of course they could not hear, they ripped me from seam to seam. At least I thought I was able to hold them back with the strength of my stitching but to my horror they produced a knife and slit my arteries that kept my being together. My legs below the knee were severed!

I was horrified as I saw my legs thrown on the fire. They firstly sizzled manfully but then began to pop and glow until they turned orange and then red and eventually the grey of finality. They were gone. I was a cripple with no legs. The girls seemed happy with their work and tossed me casually onto the pile of garments.

I was totally devastated after my terrible ordeal and lay in the dirt suffering in anguish. Most of the garments were understanding and spent the night giving comforting words but that made no difference. I had lost a part of me and had had to sit and watch it burn and I knew the torment of such a cruel torture would live with me forever. The denims were of course of no comfort and just told me to sort myself out and get on with my life. I whined that I had no life left and I was finished but they laughed at my misery and joked at my pain.

Expecting the worst I was surprised the next day when I was again seconded by my comrade and worn with obvious pride. He seemed pleased with my disfigurements and showed everyone my new look.

After a while and comforted by my comrade's pleasure I came to terms with not having legs and as my owner was so proud of me that pride soaked me with a strength of survival and I held together for some time.

As time went by I became aware that not all was right with me. I was now old and my seams were beginning to split and where my legs had been amputated I was beginning to fray. My worst moment was one day as he squatted at a council meeting. My cloth, now well worn, revealed my comrade's equipment! Clearly, no gentlemen present was prepared to comment on such a misfortune but when the young girls began to point and giggle, a whispering started. I was discarded, not for the fire but, in recognition of my will power my comrade insisted I was still of some use and I could tell he had developed a fondness for me. I was carefully folded and at his next visit to the sales he fondly deposited me in a pile with other clothes. I was not foolish enough to hope that in my aged state I would be recycled into another important person's garment but I believed that I could be of some use.

It was thus that I was surprised to find that no interest was shown in any of us during the sale and at the end of the day we were simply tossed into a large metal box and a lid sealed us in. It was soon, I believe, we were hauled on a lorry and moved along a bumpy track, jostling us all. I must say I was more than aware of the condition of my comrades and did not feel very positive about my future. I tried to take stock of my surroundings amongst the jumble of clothes wrapped round me and quickly became aware of the sounds. There was constant moaning and whining with some even screaming and others just sobbing continuously. I was almost smothered by a large faded blouse who I am sure under other circumstances could have told some quite revealing stories about her life, bearing in mind the extensive amount of female chest she must have covered during her lifetime. At present however her soft moaning was suddenly interjected by a loud wail making my seams stiffen with shock. I tried talking gently and slowly prized a conversation from her.

"We are all to be burned alive," she sobbed, "screwed up and tossed onto a continuous fire of never ending destruction. Our lives will end in torment, ashes to ashes, dust to dust," she wailed like an evangelical preacher predicting the end of the world. I was sure she was being melodramatic but her fears appeared to be regurgitated by many of my fellow passengers. My mind did not allow such dismal thoughts but my future did not seem quite as bright as I had hoped.

I used the movement of the truck to move away from my wailing mama and found myself up against a particularly shabby and malodourous pair of denims. Now I know that denims are extremely tough and therefore expected something more boisterous from them. It was thus that I was surprised to find them sobbing into their zips like the whining cowards I had often guessed they were. I started to move on but found they were gripping me pleading for my help. It seems that even at my age and my advanced state of decay my superior breeding showed. They believed that I would be able to save them from this dreadful imagined fate but, to my shame, I simply pushed them to one side and moved on. I made no attempt at conversing with them or, as my conscience later reminded me, consoling them. The journey rolled on for what appeared to be days and days without me making any further contacts. I rolled myself into a ball and contemplated my past whilst trying to ignore my future.

Eventually we stopped and we found ourselves tipped out onto a nice clean concrete surface. We all brightened with the new fresh light and the apparent consideration shown by our new masters. It seemed our future was decided and we were sorted into various piles awaiting our new direction. The sobs and screams started again as trousers were separated from their jackets or underwear. Shirts were prized apart from their close companions and the whole misery started again. Each pile was moved off into various waiting areas and I became aware of a different sort of tension. Things were happening around us that created a sense of extreme fear. Suddenly the smell hit us and it did not take long to realise it was the smell of burning cloth. Then there were the screams as we saw pile after pile of perfectly able clothing tossed uncaringly into the flames. The sight was appalling as we waited for our own brutal end.

My pile however did not move so, after a while, we hoped that we were saved from the flames. Indeed this was the case, as a group of overalls selected one item at a time and examined them closely. Suddenly the horror started and items were literally torn apart. Arms were ripped off, collars were discarded, legs were dismembered and even lapels were separated from their comrades.

The terrifying screams of horror and pain added to the sobbing of the remaining garments and my anguish was complete.

It was then that I remembered my long forgotten baptism and the strength of will and calm it gave me. I took a deep breath and calmed my seams and stiffened my zip. I was going to survive this and no orange overall was going to destroy me.

My turn came and I was grabbed and stretched and my stumps of legs were tugged, but my faith held and I remained as one. My torturer was clearly impressed by my strength and soon gave up his efforts and discarded me onto a rather small pile. It was thus that the final part of my life was to start, my third age, and my last journey. I made it clear in my mind that I would not fight this but deal with whatever problems my new life would throw at me. I had become a dish rag!

Life as a Rag

At the end of a long day when we had all been carefully rinsed and hung to rest and dry we would hang about reminiscing about our past lives. At this point the specially made ones would make jokes at our expense and laugh at our stories. Our many years' experience however enabled us to quell such youthful enthusiasm with a few well-chosen words and silence them to a hangdog sullenness. On the occasions that they continued in their turbulent ways the denims amongst us would see to it that they suffered the next day. This was not a solution with which I was comfortable, being of the more gentlemanly attitude, but denims will be denims and they did quieten the upstarts.

One of my closest friends was originally a Gieves and Hawkes, still stiff and serviceable but getting very much towards the end of his useful life. I always tried to hang around with him and listen to his stories. His gentleman was, of course, army and as such the gentleman treated him with great respect. He was kept clean and pressed and not over worked, like many a trouser. I gasped at the acquaintances he boasted from Jermyn Street and even shoes from Lobbs, made from the gentleman's personal last built and rebuilt as the gentleman changed shape.

His gentleman was of course retired by the time my friend was created but an officer always has respect for his attire and thus he enjoyed many years of useful and pleasant service. Indeed, even when he was passed on he was kept together as a suit and although not kept in such a regimental sharpness still enjoyed a gentleman's care. In his later life he suffered many painful experiences but his good breeding and stiff resolve in his developing years helped him to weather his changing fortunes and arrive at the pragmatic twilight of his existence.

As I consider my past I accept I am now a dish cloth, well treated, clean and respected. I work with many other cloths of varied origins but we get on well and are treated kindly. We are kept clean, essential for our task, and hung neatly at the end of our working day. My story covers a number of years as most of those of my colleagues do. There are a few who have been created for such a task but they are of little consequence and are not important for my tale. Many of my present comrades have lived such exciting lives, have travelled far and achieved many things. Most are contented with their process of living and the specially made ones know nothing else and in their arrogance will soon see the error of their ways.

We were all friends as we worked together, well almost together, every day. We each had different jobs which, at our age certainly, took its toll on our lifespan. There were many of my friends with whom I had spent pleasant times discussing their past and enjoying their stories. Sometimes I would find them absent at the next morning's work muster and realise their life was over, worked to their end, falling into a heap of dereliction and degradation, no longer of use for work and discarded forever.

The denims were a tough bunch and rather low on the intellect scale but they worked hard and managed to deal with all the rough tasks that were thrown at them with barely a sound of complaint. We had all tried to be friends with them but they did not want to know. Some had attempted to get closer to my pink friend, Rachel, but she was tough enough and certainly worldly wise enough, to rebuff them at every squelchy move.

There was one particular member of our workforce who was always aloof. We knew little of him despite the fact that he worked harder than most. He always seemed to be alert and ready for anything into which he was thrown. Sometimes he would disappear in the middle of the night and not be seen for days. He was khaki and stiff, silent and tough. He would have nothing to do with us mere ordinary workers. It was only late one night, when he was more forthcoming than usual, that he quietly confided in me that he was 'special sauces'. I had no idea what this meant but clearly it was important and secret. Judging by the condition he was often in on returning from such forays his tasks were extreme. He was clearly a very brave cloth.

I am at the end of my useful life, in fact quite probably at the end of my life. Disintegrating, suffering the effects of over use of detergents and turning to rubbish, an inevitable end. I must say, from what I hear, my life could have been much worse. I have had a good and varied existence, not all perfect but as I look back I am proud of the way I have performed my tasks. I remember with the fondness that the passing of time sorts into good and bad experiences, sifting the memory into a settled comfort.

23278203R00074

Printed in Poland
by Amazon Fulfillment
Poland Sp. z o.o., Wrocław